THE DOOMSDAY CIPHER

(An Avalon Adventure)

Rob Jones

Copyright © 2020 by Rob Jones

All rights reserved. No part of this publication may be used, reproduced, distributed or transmitted in any form or by any means, electronic, mechanical, photocopying, recording or otherwise, without the prior written permission of the author or publisher, except in the case of brief quotations embodied in critical reviews and certain other non-commercial uses permitted by copyright law.

THE DOOMSDAY CIPHER is a work of fiction. All names, characters, places and occurrences are entirely fictional products of the author's imagination or are used fictitiously. Any resemblance to current events or locales, or to persons living or dead, is entirely coincidental.

This book is sold subject to the condition that it shall not, by way of trade or otherwise, be lent, re-sold, hired out or otherwise circulated in any form of binding or cover other than that in which it is published and without a similar condition including this condition being imposed on the subsequent purchaser.

ISBN: 9798686719682

Other Books by Rob Jones

The Joe Hawke Series
The Vault of Poseidon (Joe Hawke #1)
Thunder God (Joe Hawke #2)
The Tomb of Eternity (Joe Hawke #3)
The Curse of Medusa (Joe Hawke #4)
Valhalla Gold (Joe Hawke #5)
The Aztec Prophecy (Joe Hawke #6)
The Secret of Atlantis (Joe Hawke #7)
The Lost City (Joe Hawke #8)
The Sword of Fire (Joe Hawke #9)
The King's Tomb (Joe Hawke #10)
Land of the Gods (Joe Hawke #11)
The Orpheus Legacy (Joe Hawke #12)
Hell's Inferno (Joe Hawke #13)
Day of the Dead (Joe Hawke #14)
Shadow of the Apocalypse (Joe Hawke #15)
Gold Train (Joe Hawke #16)
The Last Warlord (Joe Hawke #17)

The Avalon Adventure Series
The Hunt for Shambhala (Avalon Adventure #1)
Treasure of Babylon (Avalon Adventure #2)
The Doomsday Cipher (Avalon Adventure #3)

The Hunter Files
The Atlantis Covenant (Hunter Files #1)
The Revelation Relic (Hunter Files #2)
The Titanic Legacy (Hunter Files #3)

The Cairo Sloane Series
Plagues of the Seven Angels (Cairo Sloane #1)

The Harry Bane Thriller Series
The Armageddon Protocol (A Harry Bane Thriller #1)

The Jed Mason Series
The Raiders (Jed Mason #1)

The Bill Blake Series
An action-thriller series for fans of
Jack Reacher and Jason Bourne

The Operator (Bill Blake #1)
Against The Machine (Bill Blake #2)

The DCI Jacob Mystery Series
The Fifth Grave (A DCI Jacob Mystery)
Angel of Death (A DCI Jacob Mystery)

Visit Rob on the links below
for all the latest news and information:

Email: robjonesnovels@gmail.com
Twitter: @AuthorRobJones
Facebook: www.facebook.com/RobJonesNovels/
Facebook Reader Group: ADVENTURE HQ
Website: www.robjonesnovels.com

For Boo

THE DOOMSDAY CIPHER

PROLOGUE

July 1559, Mayan Empire

The Dominican friar from northern Spain struggled against his bonds, desperate to free his trembling hands from the leather straps that held them behind his back. The horror unfolding before his eyes, high in the temple at the top of the pyramid, had shaken him to his core. Thousands of miles from his homeland and surrounded by the strange and mysterious Mopan tribe, he knew this time there would be no escape from the violent and bloody fate that awaited him.

He muttered another prayer. But for all his prayers, Fray Alfonso Montesino still had his doubts about the afterlife and his place within it. When he heard the mangled screams of Fray Juan Lopez at the top of the pyramid's vertex, he knew any doubts either of them had about the hereafter would soon be settled once and for all.

All around him, Maya warriors screamed and whooped, and above their cries, a piece of sinister, primal music began thumping in the murky twilight. Still trying to wrench his hands apart, Montesino looked over to the eastern base of the pyramid and saw the musicians. They were walking in single file, playing wooden flutes and clay trumpets and banging kettle drums and shaking golden pellet-bell rattles for the god of death. A man with a flint knife joined them and led the somber procession toward the pyramid.

One by one, they made their way up the wide stone steps leading to the top of the colossal pyramid where burning torches lit the temple. The sound of the sacrifice song and the cries of the revelers mingled with the calls of some exotic birds high in the canopies of the ceiba trees behind him. Seeing his friend and colleague screaming for his life as the ritual drew nearer, Alfonso fought hard to keep his last meal down but failed. Leaning over, he threw up all over the sand at the base of the giant structure.

As the men ascended the steps, drawing closer to the top, the musicians played faster. The flutes chirped and yelped, and the drums banged harder and harder. The pellet bells rattled like angry snakes. They stripped Juan of his clothes, leaving him totally naked in the low evening light. Working to the meticulous rhythm of the drumbeat, the men dipped crude brushes into clay pots and began painting their victim a rich, vibrant blue. They made this *azul maya* color by crushing the leaves of the *añil*, a kind of indigo, and mixing them with clay. Alfonso had seen it used many times before, including for sacrifices, but never had he dreamed it might end up being painted on him and his old friend and mentor.

"*Por esta santa unción y por Su bondadosa misericordia te ayude el Señor por la gracia del Espíritu Santo para que...*" The hurriedly whispered words fell from Alfonso's lips like dead leaves blowing on the levant winds back on his Spanish farm. He had uttered the Last Rites more times than he was able to remember, but this was the first and last time he would say them for himself and his dying friend. As he finished the sacred words, the moment overcame him and he began to sob. "*...libre de tus pecados, te conceda la salvación y te conforte en tu enfermedad.*"

The men tied his friend down on the sacrificial altar

and stepped away from him. Then the priest began to chant and cry a mantra over and over, arms raised to the heavens and the flint knife gripped in his hand. What happened next, Alfonso saw with his own eyes, but he did not believe it. When a religious man saw a heathen priest summon a god to make the clouds swirl in circles, raise the wind, and pelt a tropical landscape with hailstones, he knew believing in his own god was for fools.

The Maya priest chanted louder, raising his hands further into the heavens. Imploring his pagan sky god to accept the sacrificial corpse on the altar, he waited for an answer. When it came, the young Spanish friar swallowed his doubts and prayed louder to his own god to spare him from the barbaric horror he was seeing on this terrible day.

Then the priest plunged the sharpened stone blade into his friend's stomach and ripped it open. Juan screamed, but his terrified cries were muffled by the blood flowing up through his throat. The priest tore at his body again and again, slicing thick, rugged gouges into his painted flesh as the storm grew wilder around them.

Alfonso was horrified. He witnessed the evil, depraved chanting and crazed dancing in circles, and in the sky, the storm grew stronger. The hailstones grew in size, almost as big as a man's fist. The power of the wind increased tenfold, scratching at the tops of the palms and tearing their leaves off. To save themselves, the men around the altar dropped to their knees and grabbed hold of its thick, stone legs. As they fought the strength of the storm, it increased yet again.

This time, the palm tree trunks were wrenched from the earth and flung like pinewood splinters across the complex. Some smashed into sculptures and others ripped through the thatched roofs of the villagers' dwellings. Above, the sky darkened further, churned by the growing violence of the divine storm. Alfonso had never seen anything like it, but the men around him knew what it was and had a name for it.

It was a warning from *Hurakán*.

A hurricane.

The god of storms was angry. Their offering was not good enough and they had enraged him with their disrespect. Perhaps increasing the offering might appease the great sky god of storms? Alfonso's skin crawled when he saw the men turn and look at him. The priest screamed from the top of the pyramid in the howling gale.

The words were in Mayan, but Alfonso knew they could mean only one thing.

"Bring him!"

They grabbed his arms and dragged him over to the steps. This time, there was no dancing or singing or music. This time there was only a desperate fear in the faces of the tribesmen around him, and perhaps the faintest glimmer of hope that sacrificing the second friar might be enough to appease mighty Huracan.

He summoned all his strength and screamed for his life. "No!"

Looking up the steps, he saw the priest, arms still raised to the sky and muttering a hypnotic mantra up to the racing black clouds above his head. Hailstones smashed down, one striking Alfonso's shoulder and making him cry out loud in pain. Then another hit the head of one of the men dragging him and breaking open his skull. He crashed down to the ground and the other men screamed in terror and fled, desperate to escape the brutal vengeance of the storm god. The priest screamed at them to stop, but his pleas fell on deaf ears and they scattered into the forest like frightened rabbits, leaving Alfonso unguarded in the chaos.

He knew his shoulder had been badly wounded by the

massive, sharp hailstone, but that was the least of his worries. Standing alone at the base of the pyramid, he looked up and saw only the priest. He was taking cover from the hailstones beneath a stone overhang above the altar, and Juan's savagely desecrated body was hanging off the altar, his broken limbs jutting out at awkward, sickening angles.

There was no hope for his old friend from Salamanca, but Alfonso still had a chance. If he acted quickly. With his hands still tied behind his back and pain throbbing in his shoulder, he turned and ran down the bottom few steps of the pyramid's south side. He scanned the area and saw the rainforest was the best place to disappear completely from the terrified tribe behind him.

Dodging the hailstones, he weaved through the huts and alleys until reaching the jungle and then ducked inside the treeline. His chest burned with the strain of the sprint, but he was out of sight and safe for now. He fought to control his breathing and slow his pounding heart, but then he saw something that made it beat even harder in his chest. Something which made him question all over again everything he believed about the world and the heavens above it.

As the priest's chants grew louder and he raised his tattooed arms, still dripping with Juan's blood, high into the air, the hailstorm intensified again in strength and power. The old shaman began twirling his bloody arms in a circle above his head, and as he did so a giant twister appeared in the sky above the temple, as if in response to the priest's will as if the storm were obeying his mystical chants and movements.

The storm was now more powerful than anything Alfonso had ever witnessed. A vast, swirling gray maelstrom of flashing thunderbolts and howling winds and hailstones like fists rained down all over the complex.

The priest stood at the top of the temple, calm now, almost serene as he hummed his mantra with his eyes closed and directed the raging tempest as if it were his puppet.

The storm obeyed. When the priest moved his arms one way, the eye of the storm followed. When he moved them back, it followed again. When he screamed, the winds intensified.

"Dios, ayúdame…"

But Alfonso didn't wait to see if God would help him or not. He sat down and pulled his bound hands under his backside to bring them around to his front. Then, he made the sign of the cross over his face and chest, turned on his heel, and scrambled away into the jungle. He had to get away from whatever hell he had just seen behind him, and he would run until his heart burst if that is what it took to escape this work of the devil.

1

Colorado, USA, Present Day

The dry desert air of the southern Colorado highlands moved quickly across the landscape. Warmed by the Chinook winds blowing over the eastern side of the Rockies, locals sometimes called these winds the snowkillers, because their dry, warm air melted airborne snow before it even had a chance to settle on the ground.

Carlos Mercado felt the wind on his face as he glanced up at the prison walls and watched the sky. Some looked here for evidence of God, but not this man. Today he had put his faith in something far more prosaic, but there was still no sign of his salvation anywhere in the clear blue sky, and time was getting on.

Just like his chances of getting killed. Standing here, surrounded by killers, he knew he was living on borrowed time. He had enemies. Lots of them, and they knew how to reach him, even here. The idea of fighting to stay alive for the rest of his life frightened even him, the big man. Not that he would ever tell anyone that. He tried to work out exactly what to call a place that did this to you. He decided *hell*, but it didn't matter what he called it. The United States Government called it Florence ADX, the highest security prison in the country.

This was his first year of a life sentence for murder and drug trafficking. Both him and his brother Miguel Mercado had gone down at the same trial. At least they were together, but he wasn't a young man; whatever life he had left sure as shit wasn't going to be spent in this hellhole. As the second in command of one of Mexico's most dangerous cartels, he had become accustomed to a certain way of life, and a certain standard of living. He had discovered that the US prison service didn't care about any of that. Here, he was just another inmate.

With whatever privileges he could get out of certain guards and nothing more.

One of which was paying for access to the roof, where he now stood out of sight of the watchtowers and gazed out across the Colorado horizon. Out to the west, across the plain beyond Coal Creek and over to the Wet Mountains, he watched a fat red sun sinking into a silky ribbon of ink-colored clouds.

But still no sign of his delivery from this hell.

"They're not coming. They screwed us over."

Carlos sensed his brother's fear and raised a hand. "Patience, Mico. They'll be here. We have been loyal to Tarántula and he will not forsake us."

"I hope you are right, Los."

But what if his brother was right, and they had been double-crossed? What if this was just an elaborate ruse to coax them out of the safe places they burned up their time in, and out into the yard, out into the open? Could Tarántula be trusted? They had kept quiet at the trial and protected him, but they still knew enough to lock up their notorious boss for a hundred years. Maybe he had decided to have them silenced forever?

He scanned the faces of the other prisoners out on exercise time. Most were tattooed, some almost completely. Many had thick scars on their faces. Some looked almost normal, just like the man who laundered their money for them back in Mexico City.

But they all had murder in their eyes.

As if his will had moved them, three men from the

corner of the yard turned and walked in his direction. He nudged Miguel in the ribs. "You know those guys?"

Miguel shook his head and took a step in front of his older brother. "No, they're nothing to do with me. They're pulling knives. I think this is the end, brother. Tarántula has ordered our executions to protect himself from the law. But we fight all the way down."

"It's the end, all right, Mico, but not for us." Carlos nudged his chin into the sky behind Miguel. "Our ride is here."

"Really? I don't see it."

A tiny speck on the horizon grew larger until it slowly turned into a helicopter. It descended until it was barely a few feet off the ground, but still flying at full speed. A spiraling wake of peach-colored dust billowed out behind the aircraft as it raced across the arid highlands to the west of the prison.

"I told you Tarántula would not betray us. Our loyalty to him is being repaid."

Up on the wall, just outside one of the watchtowers, a guard saw the chopper rapidly approaching the prison and ran inside to hit the alarm. The siren screamed out across the yard and the prisoners were ordered inside. Most turned and walked toward the main building, but Carlos, Miguel, and the three men with knives ignored the order.

"The assassins are still coming for us, brother," Miguel said. "Whoever they are."

"Then they are fools."

The chopper flashed over the prison's western perimeter and hovered above the yard. Guards were now all over the outer walls, backed up by other officers armed with more powerful rifles on the roof of the main building. They opened fire on the chopper, but they were badly outgunned.

The helicopter spun around and a man wearing a

bandana, sitting behind an M134 Minigun sprayed a brutal burst of fire at the armed guards now taking up a defensive position on the roof, cutting them to shreds. The guards gasped, dropped their rifles, and clutched their chests. The wounds were fatal. They tumbled over the railing at the top of the watchtower and smashed into the ground face-first.

Across the yard on the outer wall, the other prison officers never flinched, but their weapons were no match for the rotating barrel assembly currently spitting bottlenecked rifle rounds at them from its six barrels. Hell delivered to your doorstep at nearly three thousand feet per second. The barrage cut through the guards at the front of the platform, chewing holes in their bodies and blasting them over the railing.

Down in the yard, the men with knives broke into a sprint toward the brothers. Don't bring a flick knife to a heavy machinegun fight, Carlos thought. He could only guess how much money these men had been paid to kill him if they would continue their mission in these circumstances. Yet this was no time for complacency; those blades would slice him open just as fast whether there was a helicopter above him or not.

"We must go, brother!" Miguel said, tugging at his brother's arm.

"I know." He curled his lip and shouted at the men. "You will die for your attempt on my life. Dogs!"

Carlos and Miguel sprinted across the yard toward the chopper. As they drew nearer, the terrific noise of the whirring rotors combined with the electric motor driving the Minigun's rotary breech to produce an almost impossibly loud roar. Carlos ducked his head as he reached the helicopter. As he stepped up onto the skid, a hand shot out of the cool, dark interior and grabbed him, pulling him up into the cabin. Miguel was next, deftly hopping up over the skid.

Carlos laughed. "It's good to see you, Luis!"

"And you, Los."

When both men were inside, Luis called through the comms. "All onboard, get us out of here."

Carlos felt the Bell JetRanger lift up and then lurch over to the right as it caught a gust of wind coming off the high desert to the west. The pilot leveled off and pulled up sharply, crossing the yard and swooping over the main prison wall. Below, the guards emptied their weapons at the chopper, but the man at the Minigun raked them once again, cutting their bodies to ribbons.

"Good work, Héctor," Carlos said. "I see you have not lost your sense of purpose."

Héctor shrugged. "I just like killing people."

"I know you do, my old friend. I know you do. But now I need to use your toy."

"Be my guest."

The three assassins had aborted their mission when the brothers had reached the chopper, and now they had dropped the knives and were sprinting across the yard with their hands in the air, desperate for the guards not to take them out.

The surviving guards were focussing on the chopper but Carlos had the assassins in his sights. Swiveling the powerful Minigun around, he opened fire. The bullets ripped into the ground behind the fleeing men, effortlessly catching up with them, the rounds pocked the yard and kicked up tiny clouds of dust. Seconds later, the bullets found their target and ripped all three men to pieces, punching great, thick bloody holes in their backs and legs.

Carlos swung the gun around, took his hand off the trigger, and called out to the pilot. "Go."

The chopper lurched away and swooped down over the

outer wall.

Turning to his brother, he said, "Are you scared, Mico?"

Miguel shook his head. "Are you?"

"No. I am excited." He held out two gnarled, leathery hands. "Soon, Tarántula will have the power of the gods in his grasp and we will be right there beside him. Then, entire governments will fall to their knees and beg us for mercy." He licked his lips and watched the high desert scratch past beneath the speeding chopper. "But I am sad, Mico, for I have no mercy to show them."

Miguel looked at his brother and felt his skin crawl.

2
Yuriria Convent, Guanajuato, Mexico

Professor Selena Moore of the London Museum of Archaeology stepped out of the day's blistering heat and into the shade of the convent's shadowy *porteria*. Slipping off her sunglasses, she dropped them in her pocket, loosened her linen blouse, and glanced up at the crumbling plaster above her head.

Every inch of the honey-colored stonework around her was a testament to the quality of the four-hundred-year-old religious building's quality and grandeur, as were the flagstones she walked on, worn smooth by centuries of use. Turning to her father, Professor Atticus Moore, the two of them shared an excited smile.

"I can't believe this is happening, Dad."

"Believe it, Lena," he said. "And you deserve it, too. You've worked hard for this moment."

She leaned forward and kissed him on the cheek. "So have you."

"We'd better hurry along," he said, quickening his pace. "Otherwise poor old Pepe will have another attack of the vapors."

She giggled, looking ahead at Dr. Felipe Acosta as he rushed one of the convent's officials along the barrel-vaulted cloister. To their right, a bright green central courtyard surrounded by flourishing tropical pot plants was filled with the chatter of exotic, colorful songbirds.

"There are two floors," Acosta said casually. "On the ground level are the common rooms and then above them are the living quarters."

Selena gazed about at the sunlight on the far side of the Gothic arcade. "It's beautiful."

"The weather helps," Atticus grumbled. "I checked the BBC before we came out and there's another week of rain planned for London."

"I like the rain," she said defensively. "But this *is* beautiful."

"Like a paradise on Earth," Acosta ventured. "And remember, much of this place was badly affected by a great fire in the early nineteenth century, including much of the interior. Many of the murals were ruined forever at the time, so what you see is only a part of the true magnificence that once was. Come, the best is through here!"

With the rich call of a mockingbird behind them in the courtyard, they moved inside the monastery, and Selena was struck by the beauty of an enormous fresco adorning the far wall. Acosta had finished talking with the official and now turned to her and Atticus. Seeing their interest in the fresco, he took a step back and joined in their admiration.

"It depicts the Slaughter of the Innocents." His mellow Mexican accent echoed in the large stone room. "As originally described in the Gospel According to St. Matthew."

"This place just gets more and more amazing," Selena said.

Atticus nodded dreamily. "Indeed."

Acosta clasped his hands in front of him. "It is a shame we must break through it to reach the chamber."

Selena and her father had the same reaction. "You

can't be serious?" Atticus said. "Surely the convent authorities would never allow such destruction! I know I won't be a party to it."

Acosta laughed. "Relax, I am just making a joke. How is it you say – I am pushing your legs?"

"It's pulling," Selena said. "And by the way – *ha, ha, ha.*"

"Sorry, just my little sense of humor," Acosta waved the moment away. "According to the official I was speaking with moments ago, we can access the chamber through the vestry, which is just around this corner. I promise there will be no need for hammers, chisels, or any type of explosives, but we will have to lift part of the floor."

"Thank heavens for that," Atticus said, with his traditional full eyebrow raise. "If there's one thing I hate more than excitement, it's noise."

"You can imagine what his parties are like!" Riley Carr said with a smirk.

Hearing her ex's voice, Selena turned and saw him walking up behind them. The rest of the crew were beside him. Mitch Decker, her boyfriend, Charlie Valentine, and Diana Silva. Dressed in summer shirts and straw hats and wearing sunglasses, they looked like they were on vacation.

A final corner and they stepped inside the cool, dark vestry. Acosta led them across the smooth flagstone floor until they reached the entrance to the cellar. Acosta now turned a handle hidden behind a large religious screen for centuries and walked inside. They followed him down some narrow stone steps and at the bottom, he made a generous sweeping motion with his arm as he indicated their arrival. "We are here! Years after he narrowly escaped with his life during a sacrifice ritual, this is the place where Friar Alfonso Montesino hid from a major attack by local Maya warriors. He was quite an adventurer."

Selena gazed into the cellar. Amongst piles of rubble and debris from the ancient battle, she saw the grim, hopeless place where Alfonso Montesino had hidden all those centuries ago. It was a real privilege, she knew, to see where the friar and his small entourage had hidden and prayed for their lives during the onslaught.

"It's hard to imagine a place this peaceful as once being in the middle of a warzone."

"And not just once, Selena," Acosta said. "There were several occasions when the settlements in this area, including this very convent, came under attack. It is with good reason that these places were built more like fortresses than churches or cathedrals. It's fair to say that many of the local forces did not respond well to Spanish evangelization attempts."

Atticus raised a sardonic eyebrow. "That's putting it mildly, Pepe."

"Indeed it is, my friend, and yet over nine million native people were converted to Catholicism in less than a century."

Riley whistled. "That's a lot of Bibles. Who got the publishing contract?"

Acosta gave him a disapproving look. "As you know, the Franciscans worked mostly in the northern parts of Mexico, and also partly in the central regions, but the southern regions were generally controlled by the Dominicans." He paused and looked around the cellar. "Montesino was a good Dominican."

She followed Acosta and her father further down a temporary ramp and stepped into another world, where the politics of sixteenth-century conquest had wiped out a modest contingent of friars, but also several dozen local warriors. This was a time riven by hatred and the brutal conflict between empire and tribal nation.

In the damp gloom of the cellar, she heard her father speaking quietly. "This is astonishing, Pepe. Truly remarkable. It seems morbid to mention it, but some of these human remains are in very good condition. Their clothes are almost as they must have been on the day of the battle."

The man from the University of Veracruz nodded sadly and brought his hands up to his hips as he surveyed the remains littering the flagstone flooring. Leathery skin stretched taught over skulls by the dry, stable conditions of the cellar, skeletal hands reaching out from the musty-smelling monks' robes as if begging for help. "They will, of course, all be identified and returned to their families for a proper burial."

"Yes, and quite right too," Selena said. "Heaven only knows what these people must have gone through in the last few moments of their lives."

"And yet Alfonso managed to escape with his life?" Decker said.

"Yes, he did," Acosta said. "He saw an opportunity to flee and he seized it, leaving his personal possessions behind here in this place. He was subjected to a great deal of criticism when he returned to Spain. Some accused him of being too aggressive with the local tribes, and his journey into the Belize jungle was considered by many, perhaps even the King of Spain, to be a serious mishandling of his original brief."

"And your opinion?" Decker asked.

Acosta grinned at him. "I think he was a very brave man, perhaps even a little foolhardy, to do what he did. After all, if it weren't for his exploration of the deeper jungles, we would never know about all of the treasures and artifacts and rituals he described."

"And talking of which," Atticus said, slapping his

hands together and greedily rubbing them back and forth with barely contained jubilation. "I think it's time we went down inside the new part of the excavation and took a look at it, don't you?"

Neither Selena nor Acosta could think of a single reason to disagree.

3

The large flagstone tiles were harder to lift than they had thought, so after another short debate about the ethics of desecrating a four-hundred-year-old church, Dr. Felipe Acosta eventually got his way and the decision was made to break and lift one of the tiles. Both he and Atticus Moore knew it was the easiest way of accessing the crypt below the cellar, but they had disagreed about the best way forward.

"Okay, then let's do it," said Acosta. A few moments passed while a pickaxe was sourced and then Riley went to work. Half a dozen swings later, the Australian was pulling the broken flagstone segments away from the floor to reveal a flat, dusty wooden trapdoor.

Acosta gasped. "This is the door Montesino described in his memoirs!"

Atticus looked like he was falling in love all over again. "Then we found it. We finally found where he left his possessions behind. Somewhere in here, we should find the Montesino Codex, including untold information about undiscovered archaeological sites all over the region. This truly would be the greatest find of all!

"Think of the implications!" Acosta said. "This is a very special moment, my friends."

They opened the trapdoor to reveal a small chamber, no larger than a modern elevator. Inside was dumped a hessian sack. Riley sat down and swung his feet over the edge, then lowered himself down and reached for the sack. Holding it at arms' length, Decker took hold of it and placed it on the ground.

"Professor?" he said, looking at Selena. "I believe the pleasure is yours."

Selena opened it up and gasped when she looked inside. Pulling out a large, leather-bound book, her hands began to tremble with excitement.

Acosta swallowed hard and a bemused smile crossed his lips. "My God, this really is the Montesino Codex!"

Atticus hadn't heard the Mexican professor's words; he was too mesmerized by the dusty leather-bound book in his daughter's trembling hands. "We actually found it."

Selena looked at him, the look on her face told the world she was as excited about the discovery as her father. "We found it, Dad."

"May I?" he asked.

She handed him the book and he ran his fingers over the old, worn leather binding. "And what superb condition, as well! It's hard to believe this is almost five hundred years old." He began to chuckle.

"What is it, Dad?"

Slowly, Atticus started to do a little ad-libbed dance of joy on the spot. "I beat Danvers! I actually beat Danvers to the Montesino Codex."

"Who the hell is Danvers?" Decker asked.

"Nathaniel Danvers," Selena said. "He's a top-flight Canadian archaeologist working at Harvard University. Also, very rich thanks to a massive inheritance he received a few years ago and some very canny private investments. He's been looking for the Montesino Codex for ten years."

"And I beat him to it!" To everyone's relief, the dance had now ended, leaving a red-faced Atticus Moore clutching the old book to his chest as if it were a newborn baby.

"I guess he's not going to be too happy about it, am I right?" Decker said.

"Not too happy?" Atticus laughed again. "He's going to be absolutely livid! The silly sod's been searching in the wrong places all these years. First in the cathedral in Tlaxcala and then in Spain, thousands of miles away!"

"Why?" Charlie asked. "That doesn't sound top-flight to me."

"His earlier research led him to believe that after his time spent in Tlaxcala, Alfonso Montesino returned with the Codex and the rest of his belongings to his hometown of Terrassa in Catalonia. Poor old Danvers spent years trawling through the archives in the cathedral vaults in Tlaxcala until he found evidence suggesting Alfonso had indeed returned to Spain and taken the Codex with him."

"Then he arranged an extended sabbatical with Harvard to go and work in Terrassa to continue his search," Acosta said.

"And the stupid bugger is still there to this day," Atticus said, still glowing.

Acosta was more sympathetic. "His determination to find the Codex is legendary in the academic community. He is completely convinced Montesino witnessed some kind of supernatural act somewhere in Mexico and left clues about it in his memoirs. He claims the friar wanted to tell the world about what he had seen but was so terrified by it, he created some sort of cipher which he included in this Codex. Our discovery of this today will upset him a great deal."

"Danvers has a large and vivid imagination," Atticus said. "The truth is the real value of the Codex is that it should reveal a great cache of Maya relics and treasures which Montesino also referred to in his memoirs when safely back in Spain."

"Either way, our discovery of this today will upset him an awful lot!" Acosta said.

"Upset him?" Atticus said, setting the Codex down on

top of the bag. "It'll break him! Lena dear, would you please take a picture of me holding it and then send it to him on that little phone of yours?"

"No."

"Pretty please?"

"No."

"Mitch?"

"Leave me out of it."

"Anyone?"

"Maybe later," Riley finally said. "But I think right now we have more important things to worry about than you breaking poor old Danvers."

"Riley's right," Decker said. "It's costing money to park the Avalon at Francisco Mujica Airport. You do realize that, right?"

Selena said, "I thought you said they waived the fees if we were refueling there?"

"I did. We're not refueling there."

"Ah."

"We refueled in Barbados. Remember?"

"How could I ever forget Barbados," she said dreamily. "That night on the beach was…"

Atticus clamped his hands over his ears. "All right, keep it down – Father Alert."

"Sorry, Dad."

"Yeah, and ex-boyfriend alert too," Riley said. "Keep that stuff for your alone time, kids."

During the banter, Diana Silva had quietly picked up the Montesino Codex in her usual discreet way and was gently turning the fragile pages. As the others traded barbs and jokes, her eyes danced over the faded writings of the long-dead friar. She had little problem understanding the text; most was in Latin, in which she was fluent, and the rest was in slightly archaic Spanish. Being a first-language Portuguese speaker, this also presented only a small challenge but after a few moments, a frown darkened her slim face.

"I think I might have found something here."

4

The Avalon crew and Acosta stopped talking and looked over at the small figure sitting on a wooden chair with the Codex in her lap.

"What have you found?" Selena asked.

"I think your friend Danvers might have been right after all."

Atticus stared at her, unblinking "What do you mean?"

"About what Montesino saw all those hundreds of years ago."

"Impossible," Atticus said. "Danvers said Montesino witnessed some kind of divine force. As a trained, professional archaeologist and a man of science, I refuse to believe such nonsense."

"What makes you say this, Diana?" Decker said.

"I'm not sure where to start, but here he talks about being filled with terror at the hands of a pagan god."

"Not a good start," Charlie said.

Riley's smile faded. "But there's still treasure, right?"

Selena sighed. "Please, go on, Diana."

The Portuguese woman was quiet for a while, studying the text. She mumbled to herself as she followed her finger along one of the lines. As if she hadn't heard a word, she said, "And here's a reference to Ah h'in."

"Ah ha!" Riley said. "Ah h'in!"

Selena slapped him out of the way. "Stop being an idiot. What's the problem, Diana?"

"The rest of the text is straightforward enough, but I don't recognize this word."

"Ah h'in?" Atticus said, turning to the group. "What

does that mean?"

Selena peered down at the friar's spidery handwriting. "I have no idea. It certainly doesn't look like a Spanish word. More like Arabic or something. Over to you, Diana. This is your specialist field. Have another think about it."

Diana looked at the faded calligraphy of Alfonso Montesino and thought again about the strange word he had written in his journal all those centuries ago. "No, it's definitely not Spanish or Latin or even Arabic. Wait. If you look a little closer, maybe it doesn't say *Ah h'in*. If you look closely the 'h' is actually a 'k' – the lower part of the letter is very faded, almost imperceptible, but it's definitely there."

"So it's *Ah k'in*," Selena said. "Is *that* a Spanish word?"

Diana shook her head. "No."

"We are making *outstanding* progress right now folks!" Riley said, rubbing his hands together. "Easily the best treasure hunting team in the world."

"Actually, we are," Diana said with a withering glance at the Australian soldier. "On reflection, I think this word is written not in Spanish or Latin or Arabic but in Mopan."

"This is all Greek to me," Riley said.

Decker scratched his chin and sighed. "Wait a minute. What's Mopan?"

Riley sighed and shook his head. "Don't you know anything, Mitch? It's like when you're just really sad and down and, you know... *mopan* around the house."

Charlie chuckled, but the others were less amused.

"Shut up now please, Riley," Selena said. "The adults are talking."

"Yeah," Decker said. "And I still don't know what Mopan is."

"Not just what, but *who*," Selena said. "The Mopan are

a Maya people indigenous to the Yucatec peninsula and the mountains of Belize."

"And it's also the word for the Yucatecan branch of the Mayan language," Diana said. "Today it's spoken by around four thousand people in Guatemala and eight thousand people in Belize."

"But what we all want to know my dear," Atticus said, "is what does this mysterious *Ah k'in* word mean?"

"It isn't perfectly translatable, but the closest would be something between a high priest and a doctor, similar to the Taino word *behique*."

Decker considered what she had said. "So, a powerful and important figure around these parts five hundred years ago?"

Selena took over. "Absolutely, yes. These men were much more than the people we call priests today. They were a complex blend of healers, diviners, scientists, and also leaders. They usually had a very comprehensive knowledge of what today we call the Maya Katun Prophecies or Cycles."

"That's sounding more like it," Charlie said.

Riley looked across at him, confused. "It would be if I knew what she just said."

"You're referring to the Maya calendar, right?" Decker asked.

Selena took a second to consider how to explain. "The Maya calendar is a complicated business, but it's what archaeologists and anthropologists generally refer to as the Long Count, which is around one-fifth of the cycle of the precession of the equinoxes."

Now Charlie looked even more confused than Riley. "And how long is that?"

"Long. The full cycle is twenty-six thousand years, so a fifth is five-thousand, two hundred years."

"Whoa," Riley said. "That's nearly as long as it takes

to get a tax refund."

Selena ignored him. "The Maya had a very strong understanding of long timescales, much better than the average man or women does in our time. They divided time further into what they called *baktuns*, which was one-thirteenth of the Long Count, which is three-hundred and ninety-four years, and they kept accurate calendars detailing all of this."

"And these *Ah k'in* guys worked all this out just from looking at the stars?" Riley asked.

Acosta nodded. "Precisely, yes. In some respects, they were a very advanced society."

"Apart from the decapitations and ripping out of human hearts, am I right?" Charlie said sarcastically. "Or am I right?"

"I said, *in some respects*," Acosta added. "In other ways, they were of course very barbaric."

"What else does Montesino say about this high priest?" Atticus asked. "Is there anything more about what he saw?"

Diana traced her finger along the text. "He says this *Ah k'in* could speak to the gods. He mentions Huracan in particular."

"Huracan?"

"I didn't think Lamborghini made those babies until 2014?" Riley said.

Selena pursed her lips and stared at him, unsure if it was worth the effort. "Huracan as in the god of storms, wind, and fire, chuckles."

"Gotcha. I'll put it in my phone for future reference."

"Please go on, Diana," Atticus said.

"Montesino is very clear now," she said, re-reading some text. "I'm sure I haven't made a mistake but he seems to imply that the *Ah k'in* could summon Huracan at will. He writes very clearly about how he watched him call on the god and use his divine powers to annihilate a congregation worshipping at a temple. Montesino says he witnessed it with his own eyes, including the death of another friar during a sacrifice."

"My God..." Acosta said, "Danvers was right."

Atticus frowned. "Wait, he watched this priest annihilating the congregation? What does he mean by that, exactly?"

Diana scanned the text again. "He says he saw him summon Huracan and bring destruction on the temple and its worshippers. He describes how he called on Huracan and channeled a terrific storm from the sky which he was able to wield like some sort of divine power, at his will."

"Cool," Charlie said. "Cool and yet sadly completely impossible."

"That is what he writes," Diana said patiently.

"But maybe he'd one too many sherries or smoked some of the local flora when he wrote it," Riley said. "That's possible, no?"

"Maybe, but he goes further," Diana said. "He says local legend held that the *Ah k'in* was buried with the divine power of Huracan. He calls it the Doomsday Power, or the Stormbringer."

Atticus's voice was suddenly frail. "This really is the Doomsday Cipher obsessing Danvers all these years."

"Sounds inviting," Charlie said. "And in no way threatening. I like it."

"Where was the *Ah k'in* buried?" Selena asked.

"In a place called Xunantunich," she said, frowning.

"Huh?" Riley said.

"It's an ancient Maya site," Selena said. "It means Stone Woman."

Diana said, "Montesino says in the jungle to the west of the site. He gives a precise map here and some directions involving something called the Jaguar Temple and another one…" she peered closer at the manuscript… "something called the High Temple, I think. He has drawn some images here of these temples in alignment. He also says there are two entrances to the burial chamber. But I don't know where any of these things are, sorry. I'm just a translator."

"Good job we have two archaeologists in the crew then," Decker said.

Acosta raised a sheepish hand. "Three."

"Sorry, three."

"But do any of the three archaeologists know where this place is?" Charlie asked.

All three of them smiled and nodded their heads.

"Oh, yes," Selena said. "Oh yes, indeed we do! Xunantunich is a very unique site in ancient Maya culture."

"Why?" Riley asked.

"Mainly because it survived for so much longer than the other cities after the collapse of Maya civilization. A rich life went on in a bustling city there for around two hundred years after the rest of the civilization declined into collapse."

"So where is it?" Charlie asked.

"I know where it is," Decker said. "I know a guy who rents Jeeps to tourists down there."

Selena gave him a look. "How odd."

"Small world, huh?" he said.

"How long to get there in the Avalon?" she asked.

"A few hours, I guess."

"In that case, Captain Decker," Selena said, smiling, "set your compass for western Belize!"

5

Cancún, Mexico

The man they called Tarántula stared at his namesake as it crawled over the face of the dead man down at his feet. He sipped some fresh, iced water from a heavy crystal tumbler and tracked the large, hairy Mexican fireleg tarantula feeling its way over the dead man's nose, using it as a bridge to cross from one blood-stained cheek to another. He studied its movements and mannerisms with intense interest, the way it set down its legs on the man's cooling flesh, but never once before feeling its way forward with the hairy pedipalps protruding from either side of its fovea.

What would it do? Leave in disinterest, or try to consume part of it?

He pulled the half-empty bottle of Acqua di Cristallo from the top shelf of the refrigerator and unscrewed the little tin cap. The first half had been drunk with a woman the other night, mixed with American whiskey, but today it had taken on a Zenlike medicinal quality. He filled his glass and gazed around his large sunken living room. The space was filled with daylight, diffused by the tinted windows elegantly designed by himself so many years ago.

He sipped more of the refreshing water and stepped away from the dead man. Poor José had disappointed him one too many times. Never a good idea where Tarántula was concerned. He had been surprised José had called his bluff, such was the terror and fear he created in his underlings. But he had done, so he paid the ultimate price.

Turning to the man standing behind him at the door to his study, he said, "Any news from Acapulco, Rafa?"

"Not yet, boss."

He gave a shallow nod. Sipped more water and stayed calm. Fought the rage away. No news was good news, after all, and Santiago Rocha had a lot to think about. A few months ago he had double-crossed Tarántula over a drugs deal and now he was a dead man walking unless he paid the money he owed, with interest.

"They still have another twenty-four hours until the deadline."

"Yes, boss."

"And what about the Mercados?" He now turned and fixed sharp black eyes full of evil intelligence on him, as cold as desert snow. "I hear their escape was a success."

Rafael Brolo felt his skin crawl with cold fear. "A total success, boss. They're already on their way down to Mexico, but..."

"But what?" The eyes burned into him.

"I just heard from Diablo. He says a team of foreigners were at the convent. They went inside and met with one of the priests there."

Tarántula felt his blood running hotter. "What are you trying to tell me, Rafa? That months of research has all been for nothing?"

"It looks like the convent authorities have been working with this team for some time. They're archaeologists, I believe. Foreign. They found the Montesino Codex and..."

Tarántula's rage burst out of him in a deafening scream as he hurled the crystal tumbler across the room and smashed it into the wall. Brolo cowered as it shattered into a thousand pieces, taking a step back until his back brushed up against the heavy oak door.

"No!" Tarántula said. "The Snake King will kill us all if we screw this up! How could this happen?"

Brolo felt sweat beading on his forehead in the air-conditioned room. It sat on his browline for a few seconds before trickling down into his eyes. He blinked it away and swallowed hard, wiping damp palms on his suit trousers. "I... I..."

Tarántula searched the room for his twenty-four-carat gold plated Colt pistol and found it resting on the edge of his desk. He had set it down there after burying two rounds in José's chest a few short moments ago. "You need to stop talking now, Rafa. I am close to doing something I might regret. You are an old friend, after all."

"I feel the same deep rage as you, Ramon!"

Tarántula's blood now turned to ice in his veins. "What did you just call me, Rafa?"

Brolo wished he could turn to water and seep away under the gap in the door. "I'm sorry, it was just habit. From when we were kids."

"No one calls me that anymore, Rafa. You of all people understand this."

"Si, but..."

Tarántula's icy scowl broke into the faintest hint of a smile. "You are right, old friend. You must think I am some kind of monster. Insane, even. Please, forgive me."

"It's nothing, Tarántula. Nothing at all. You know how much I respect you."

"Of course. We must make preparations for the next phase of the Snake King's plan. Fetch me my pistol and we will drive out to the airport."

"Yes, boss."

Brolo walked away from the door and crossed the sumptuous study toward the desk. The view from

Tarántula's beach house was one of the most expensive in the entire city. Situated on its own stretch of private beach in the district of El Rey, the highly coveted property had once belonged to a Saudi prince and gave breathtaking views out over the dazzling turquoise waters of the northern Caribbean rim.

"This team of foreign archaeologists," Tarántula said. "I take it you had Diablo follow them?"

"Of course, boss. They took off from Bajío Airport in a private plane. He said it was a vintage plane, like something out of a museum."

Tarántula laughed. When he knew it was safe to do so, Brolo joined him.

"They fly around in a vintage plane?" Tarántula asked.

"Si."

"Not much of a match for my brand new jet!"

"No, boss."

The Embraer Lineage had recently put a seventy-five million dollar hole in one of Tarántula's offshore bank accounts, but it had all been worth it. The bespoke private jet came with a master bedroom, a shower, and skylights in the roof. It was no more than he deserved. He was the most renowned drug lord in Latin America and one of its most notorious killers. He had a reputation to maintain. He knew being the best meant being *seen* to be the best.

Tarántula picked up his pistol and caressed the smooth leaf patterns engraved in the gold plate. "A vintage plane... hilarious. What was their flight plan?"

"According to Diablo, they filed a flight plan to the Maya Flats airstrip."

Tarántula frowned. "In Belize?"

"Si."

The drug lord's mind began to whir. What was in Maya Flats? He stared down at José's corpse. The tarantula had managed to crawl up over his chin and was now making its way across his throat toward his bloodstained shirt. Maya Flats... Maya Flats...

"If this is true, it looks like these fools are leading us directly to where we need to go. I know where we must go!"

"The Snake King will be pleased, boss. Where is it?"

Still gripping the bespoke pistol, Tarántula grinned. "Somewhere very special."

6

After a long pause, he said, "It's Xunantunich! Whatever they found in the Montesino Codex has pointed them toward Xunantunich."

"The ruins?"

"Of course, the ruins. Don't be such a fool."

"I'm sorry, boss."

"Let's pray to God we can find them down there. Perhaps then the Snake King will forgive us for letting them get to the Codex before we did."

"Si."

Tarántula weighed the gun in his hand and looked up from the dead man to the sumptuous bay window on the other side of the room. White-hot sun pitched down over a neon sea busy with windsurfers and motorboats. He sniffed sharply and turned to his old friend.

"Of course, we would not need the services of God if you had done your job properly and secured the original memoirs ahead of these foreign archaeologists."

"As I said, Diablo told me that…"

He stopped speaking when Tarántula raised his Colt and aimed it at him. "I am very disappointed in you, Rafa."

"No! Please, old friend!"

Tarántula fired, planting the first round in Brolo's chest. His old friend dropped to his knees and grasped at the wound with his left hand. He reached out with his right hand to Tarántula, fingers spread. "Please… I am sorry!"

"You failed me today, Rafa. Your mistake is unforgivable."

He fired a second shot into his chest. The explosion was like thunder, but this time the bullet blasted out of his back and buried itself in the oak door behind him. A third, fourth, and fifth shot followed each one spraying blood out across the room.

Tarántula remained calm as Brolo hit the floorboards and started moaning in agony. Blood poured out onto the polished wood around him.

"What if this goes wrong, and these people find the Stormbringer before us? Now, the Snake King might lose his only chance to possess the power of the ancients. You know how that makes me feel?"

Moans and whining from Brolo. A mumbled plea for mercy was cut short by Tarántula pointing the Colt 2000 at the dying man's legs and firing off shots six, seven, and eight. The deafeningly loud explosions rocked the room, but Tarántula was not done yet.

"It makes me feel angry but also sad. Angry that one of my oldest friends could not understand how important this is to me, but so sad that now I am forced to do this."

"Please..."

Tarántula knew his weapon. He had cherished it since the day his father had given it to him when he was twelve. He had killed many men and women with it. Every night, he made sure it had a fresh, full magazine of fifteen rounds just before he slipped it under his pillow and went to sleep. José had taken two of those rounds, and now Brolo would take the other thirteen.

"Incompetent fool!"

Shots nine, ten, and eleven into the unconscious man's abdomen.

"Liar! Traitor!"

He fired the last two rounds into his head, finally putting him out of his misery. Then he hit the mag release, dumped the empty magazine, and smacked a fresh one from his desk drawer back into the gun. Then he picked up his phone.

"Get in here, Diego."

Moments later, a large man with a thick mustache and long black hair pulled into a ponytail opened the door. Despite his face being mostly covered with gang tattoos, he couldn't hide his horror when he registered the sight of the two dead men on the floor.

"I heard the gun, but I thought it best to leave you alone," he said.

"You a smart man, Diego Novarro. If you had come in here, I might have killed you, too."

Now, Novarro saw the hairy spider crawling over José's stomach. "What do you want me to do?"

"First, I want you to get this garbage out of my office. Take it down to Benicio's scrap metal yard and process it in the normal way, in the car crusher."

"Got it."

"Then, I need you to get the jet ready. Diablo says there was a team of foreign archaeologists at the convent. They're flying in a vintage plane and they just took off for Xunantunich ruins, so we still stand a good chance of beating them there if we leave at once. My jet is much faster. I feel the Snake King's eyes crawling all over me, the way this spider crawls on José's stomach."

Novarro nodded. "Yes, boss."

As Novarro began dragging Brolo's bullet-ridden corpse out of the door, Tarántula slipped his Colt into his holster, reached down, and scooped up the tarantula, now crawling on José's leg. He cradled the fat, hairy spider in his hands for a moment and then spoke, lowering his voice to the gentle whisper of a father soothing his troubled child.

"Sorry, you had to go through that, my darling. But it will all be worth it in the end. Papa is going to be much more powerful soon. Papa is going to possess the power of the ancient gods. Then, the whole world will change forever."

7

Xunantunich Ruins, Western Belize

Decker teased the throttle and brought the Avalon's engines to idle. Less than two hundred feet above the narrow Maya Flats runway and he could barely see it thanks to a powerful storm that had blown in from the sea, bringing a viciously heavy downpour onto the land. As rain streaked across the windshield and a strong gust buffeted them from the side, he struggled to bring the old plane smoothly down.

"What the hell happened to paradise?" Riley called out. He was standing in the cockpit door looking down at Decker and Selena who were strapped into their seats.

"It got lost," said Selena. "Now sit down before you fall down."

Decker sighed. "Damn it, Riley! I told everyone to sit down and buckle up. Do it now."

"Aye aye, Cap'n!"

He got to his seat seconds before the aircraft's gear touched down on the slick wet runway and Decker put the two powerful engines into reverse. They revved and roared in response and a low, loud grumble vibrated through every panel and rivet onboard.

He slammed on the brakes and brought the heavy aircraft to a thundering, juddering halt right at the very end of the runway with just inches to spare. Using the engines and rudder to turn in a giant arc on the grass, he turned the plane away from the runway, pulled the throttle back to idle, and cut the power.

Riley's face appeared once again in the cockpit door. "That was a real brown trouser job, Mitch!"

"I got us down alive, didn't I?" he said. "What more do you expect?"

Selena was still wincing. "And thanks for the imagery, Riley."

Riley slapped them both on the shoulder and peered out through the cockpit window. "Is that your mate over there by the Jeeps?"

Decker looked across the airfield. A filthy portacabin beside a small car yard with LOPEZ'S JEEPS written above it waited in the rain.

"Yes, that's Mauricio's place."

"Doesn't exactly look like he has a great choice," Selena said disapprovingly. "I can only count one."

"When I called him, he told me he had half a dozen," Decker said. "I don't understand."

"Let's go and find out then," Atticus said from just behind Riley. "And let's get on with the adventure!"

They stepped out of the Avalon into the thick, sucking Belize humidity and made their way over to the customs official. He was housed in a small building just beside the airport and after a few moments asking questions and stamping passports, he allowed the crew to walk back out into Belize and over to the rental yard.

A short man in white shorts and a black short-sleeved shirt strolled over to them with a big, toothy grin on his unshaven face. "Mitch!"

"Mauro! How are things?"

"Always good." He raised his two hands, palms up as if weighing something. "But only so long as I keep the sunshine and stress in the right balance."

Riley looked out at the rain-soaked airstrip. "Sunshine?"

"And Stress?" Charlie said. "In a place like this? Seems like paradise to me, even with the rain!"

Mauro's face darkened. "You would be surprised what can happen even in a paradise."

Decker pushed his hat an inch or two up his forehead to get a better look at his old friend and then pointed his finger at the Jeep. "Is that the only one you've got?"

"Sorry, but yes."

"But you said you had several to choose from! We have to drive out to the ruins today."

"This is not a far journey, Mitch. Just a few kilometers. No more than thirty minutes' drive."

"I know where it is," Decker affirmed. "I can read a map, Mauro. The point is, what if we need to go farther? Sometimes our investigations lead us onto other locations." He took another look at the old heap beside them. "I'm not convinced this vehicle could make it to the edge of the airfield."

"Of course, she can!"

Selena rolled her eyes. "Why do men always have to refer to machines as she?"

"It's a term of endearment," Decker said. "The Avalon is a 'she'."

"And don't I know it..."

'And just what is that supposed to mean?"

Selena opened her mouth to speak but Riley stepped in.

"I think we may be straying from the point," he said. "Which is that this Jeep is a heap of crap."

"No, it's fine," Mauro said. "I drove her in the forest reserve just south of here a few days ago. She'll do anything you want her to do with no complaints and minimal cost, except for maybe a little wear to the rubber." He kicked the tires with his tennis shoe. "I swear."

A wistful smile spread on Riley's face as he sighed. "Reminds me of a chick I once knew in Nha Trang."

"Oh, please!" Selena said with disgust. "I do wish you'd have the courtesy to keep the contents of your sordid little mind to yourself."

"You're just jealous," he said.

"I think not, Mr. Carr."

Mauro, said, "It doesn't matter one way or the other. This is the only Jeep. Take it or leave it."

"I guess we'll take it," Selena said.

"I'm sorry," Mauro added. "Men came here earlier and took the best Jeeps. The money they offered was top dollar and they threatened me. I couldn't turn them down!"

"Men, what men?" Decker asked.

"Mexicans, I think. Several tough-looking characters, lots of gang tattoos. One of them, I think it was their leader was a very strange man, but he had lots of dollars and threatened my life so I looked the other way in a hurry."

"How was he strange?"

"Something about the look in his eye maybe, I don't know. You know how these things are." He tapped his chest. "Instinct. Anyway, this really is my next best Jeep."

"It's your only Jeep," Selena said.

"It's still very good, I promise."

"Really?" Decker said. "Because it still looks like a heap of crap to me."

Atticus frowned. "Tell me more about these men though. I'm intrigued? Where is their aircraft?"

"They arrived in a chopper. Said they had flown into Belize City on a private jet and that they were a team of treasure hunters from somewhere in Mexico. They had guns, too. Lots of guns."

"Guns?" Decker said. "This sounds like trouble. I mean, why here? Why now? We find evidence that Montesino's Doomsday Machine was real and buried out in Xunantunich, and by the time we get here, a small army of men have already arrived armed to the hilt?"

"They're probably just on a hunting trip," Riley said.

"Yeah, right." Decker leaned in and picked at a flake of rust on the rear wheel arch. "Did they say where they were heading?"

Mauro nodded. "Sure, the ruins out at Xunantunich."

"Quelle surprise," Atticus said.

Decker sighed. "Great. And this is definitely your next best Jeep, right?"

"My very best," Mauro said with a grin. "I swear to you. Only the very best for Mitch Decker."

Decker straightened himself up and squared up to him. "Because if I didn't know you any better, Mauro, I'd say you reneged on the deal you made with me just to make a buck out of these guys with guns, keeping this heap of rusting junk back just for me."

"What is this?" Mauro said. "You insult me. You offend me. Your words cut me deep. How long have we known each other?"

"Seems like forever."

Mauro grinned at Selena. "Nearly ten years. That's how long. We met in the Caribbean. You want to know how much credit, trust, and faith ten years buy you?"

"Go ahead, Mauro. You tell her," Decker said, checking the tires' pressure.

"Nothing," he said. "Not with Mitch Decker. Not a thing. See how he distrusts me?"

"He has a point about the Jeep, Mr. Lopez," Selena

said. "It does seem somewhat worn."

"As I said, take it or leave."

"Gee thanks," Decker said sarcastically. "We'll take it."

8

They paid Mauro Lopez in American dollars and climbed into the old Jeep. It was a relief to get out of the rain and on their way. They took the Western Highway south to San Jose Succotz and then followed Diana's directions to make a right turn and pull up on the banks of the Mopan River.

"What's that thing?" Selena asked, pointing to a small wooden shed floating on the river.

"It's a hand-cranked ferry," Decker said. "Don't tell me you've never hand-cranked a ferry before?"

"I don't know about a ferry exactly," Riley said, "but I can tell you that when we used to go out together..."

"Thank you, Riley, and do stop being so vulgar," Selena said. "And no, I have never used one of these contraptions before. What makes you so surprised?"

Decker shrugged. "I just thought with you being an archaeologist and all you might have come across one before, that's all. No harm no foul."

"C'mon," Charlie said. "Let's pull the ferry back over to our side of the river and get on board. It's getting late and we don't want to be getting back after the bar shuts."

"And remember the men with guns," Acosta said. "Lopez said he gave them the Jeeps earlier today for their journey out to the ruins. It's already way past normal visiting hours and yet the ferry is still on the north bank. If you ask me, the armed men he's talking about are still at the ruins."

"The professor is right," Selena said. "Let's get a move on."

Decker and Riley hopped out of the Jeep and walked over to the riverbank in the torrential rainfall. The young Australian grabbed the crank handle and began to winch the small wooden ferry back over the Mopan. Decker checked up and down the tropical river for any signs of the armed men but saw nothing. When the ferry was in place, Charlie fired up the engine and drove the Jeep carefully down a slippery, muddy bank and then onto what was essentially a covered raft.

With everyone safely on board, Riley hopped up beside the Jeep and operated a second crank to wind the ferry slowly across the muddy, jade green river. The endless downpour clattered heavily on the ferry's tin roof as they drifted over to the other bank. From her seat inside the Jeep, Selena peered across the rain-pocked water at their destination and saw nothing but logwood and mahogany trees obscured in the steaming rain.

When they reached the other side, Riley secured the rope and blew out a deep breath. "Not as easy as you might think. Bloody handle has ruined my nice soft hands."

"Stop messing about and get in the car!" Selena called out from the window.

When he and Decker were safely inside, Charlie drove off the ferry and onto the north bank of the Mopan. Then he turned right and headed up a narrow track and into the trees. The steamy air surrounding the Jeep was filled with the sound of croaking toucans and rattling cicadas.

"This place gives me the creeps," Diana said.

"Not me." Selena shook her head. "I think it's beautiful."

"Yeah, it sure is," Riley said. "But if we get there and we find some gates with Jurassic Park written on them, I'm out of here."

"It's not Jurassic Park waiting for us," Atticus said.

"Look!"

They followed his pointing finger through the rain-streaked windshield and saw the incredible sight of the world-famous Xunantunich Ruins approaching at the end of the tree-lined track they were driving on.

"I still can't believe we're going to find anything here," Decker said. "If these ruins are so famous then surely they've been searched inside out by countless people over the years. Whatever the old friar thought was buried here has to have been found by now. If not by professional archaeologists then looters."

"Not necessarily," Selena said. "Even famous sites sometimes guard secret treasures for a long time without anyone ever finding them. Take Holmul, for example."

"Where?" he asked.

"It's a pre-Columbian Maya site in the Petén Basin on the border of Belize and Guatemala, first discovered by modern archaeologists from Harvard well over a hundred years ago. The city there was probably founded around 800BC and like most other places, it was abandoned around the time of the great collapse in Maya civilization."

"When was that again?" Diana asked.

"What we call the 'Classic Maya Collapse' happened around 900AD," Selena said. "And that was the end of Holmul, like most other places in their culture. But the point, in answer to Charlie's original question, is that only a few years ago a team of archaeologists discovered two tombs in Holmul full of the most amazing treasures and artifacts. Totally untouched."

"Tombs?" Decker asked. "Tell me more."

Selena grinned as Charlie drove the Jeep down the track. She always liked it when Decker showed an interest in her work. "Yes, tombs. Vaulted chambers beneath two of the pyramids in the city. There was all manner of treasures inside the tombs, including a skeleton with jade-inlays on its teeth, an honor reserved for Maya royalty. They also found ceramics, obsidian, necklaces, and other separate pieces of jade jewelry."

"Quite a find," Charlie said.

"And the point is that not only had professional archaeologists never found them, but it had also escaped looters, not only from 900AD all the way up to the find in 1911 by Professor Merwin's Harvard team, but in the intervening years from that discovery all the way up to three or four years ago. It just goes to show, there are a lot of undiscovered sites in a place like this, just waiting to be unearthed and brought to light. The treasures waiting to be discovered are unimaginable."

"All that gold!" Riley said, rubbing his hands together. "Fiji, here I come!"

"All that *knowledge*," said Selena, frowning. "And with some luck, we might make a similarly impressive discovery for ourselves today."

"Knowledge I can handle," Decker said. "Gold I can also handle. What bothers me is Montesino's doomsday surprise."

Charlie pulled up in the parking lot and switched off the engine. "Nous sommes arrivés."

"Better we find it than anyone else," Acosta said. "Especially a gang of armed men."

"Talking of whom…" Diana scanned outside her window. "Any sign of them?"

"Not that I can see," said Decker. "No sign of any of Mauro's Jeeps. Maybe they've moved on."

"I don't think so," Atticus said. "And if Danvers was right, I'm starting to understand why a gang of thugs would have an interest in this place. If there really is some kind of doomsday machine here, it's imperative we get to it first and secure it for men and women of learning.

Heaven knows what Montesino saw, but if he was halfway accurate in his description then we can be sure we don't want a gang of armed criminals reaching it before us."

"They don't have the Codex or Montesino's directions," Selena said.

Atticus gave one of his long, nervous sighs. "Of course, but it's still bothering me. I mean, what on earth would they want it for?"

"We can worry about that later," Decker said, unbuckling his seatbelt. "Right now we need to get on and find what we're looking for before they do, and that means a hike through some pretty unforgiving jungle off to the west. So let's get started or we're going to lose light."

9

They walked across the site, skirting its southern border, and made their way to the jungle off to the west. Hacking their way through the dense rainforest, they weaved a winding path around bushy breadfruit trees and wild tangles of bromeliads and spikey epiphytes. The heat was intense, and their rain and sweat-soaked bodies ached from head to toe by the time they reached the area described by Fray Alfonso Montesino in his crumbling, yellowed manuscript.

"Is this it?" Decker asked, looking around and seeing nothing but undergrowth.

They were standing in a small grove of cashew trees growing at the bottom of the slope to the complex's west, exactly where Montesino had written about. Looking up at the ruins off to their east, Selena followed the friar's code and carefully aligned the Jaguar Temple with the High Temple, or what was also known today as El Castillo, the castle. "I think a little more to the west."

Riley pulled his machete blade from the stem of a fan palm and wiped the sweat from his forehead. Turning to face the others with a grin on his face, he said, "Which way now, Lena?"

"Based on Diana's translation of the text, I think we need to keep going west for another hundred feet or so. That's where the river runs into the meander drawn by Montesino and it's also where the jungle seems to be at its heaviest. If there really is some kind of hidden burial ground around here, then it would have to be somewhere fairly impenetrable."

"Surely someone flying over it in a plane would have

seen *something*," Decker said. "And what about satellite surveillance?"

"Not nearly as extensive as you might think," Charlie said. "When I was in the Royal Military Police, I worked on a couple of jobs involving civilians in the Secret Intelligence Service. They had experience in satellite recon and told me a lot of the world is still largely uncharted, especially places like this, and especially in the sort of detail to reveal hidden entrances and so on. It's totally feasible that Montesino was telling the truth about the burial chamber."

"I can concur," Acosta said. The older man was breathing heavily. The effort of the march and the humidity of the rainforest had allied against his weary body. "Many of our greatest discoveries were in areas we thought we had mostly mapped out. So yes, it's feasible."

"Come on, let's keep going," Diana said. She had walked ahead and caught up with Riley as he hacked through the final few yards of foliage. The two of them were standing close enough to the river to hear it rushing over some rocks a little to their left. In front of them, the land sloped down into a hollow full of thick, tangled vines. "It's getting dark."

Another short walk. Each step they took, the undergrowth grew denser and harder to hack their way through. Selena stopped and looked up the slope once again. The temples were obscured even more by the rainforest now, but she was still able to see them, and this time the alignment was even better.

"Here," she said with confidence. "This is the view Montesino described in his journal. This is the place he claims the priest was buried with the Stormbringer."

"Progress," Acosta said. "At last."

"But I don't see anything," Charlie said.

Diana gasped. "Yes! Look down there!"

The others had caught them up and were gathered on the edge of the slope. "What am I looking at?" Atticus said.

Diana made her way slowly down into the foliage. "Some rocks, boulders maybe. Behind these vines."

"Look out for snakes," Riley said, stumbling down after her. "I don't want to have to suck any poison out of the bite wound."

She rolled her eyes. "I'd sooner die."

He laughed. "Sounds like you never got bitten by a snake before, mate!"

She ignored him. "Here." The Portuguese woman swept a thick fistful of vine creepers to the side to reveal a steep rockface in front of her. What had looked like natural rocks from a distance were in fact hand-carved blocks of stone built into the side of a rise. She traced her index finger along one of the grooves dividing two of the blocks and smiled.

"I think I found the entrance," she said. "Behind these vines! Look, if I move some more away you can see the outline of a door and a sort of stone handle…"

"Wait!"

Riley grabbed her arm and pulled her away. "It's a boobytrap. Check out the last dude who tried to get in here."

Now she saw it. A sun-bleached skeleton with vines twisting out of its eye sockets stared back at her from beside the wall. She gasped and staggered back into the Australian's arms.

"Take it easy," he said. "You're okay."

"Whoa," Charlie said. "Looks like we're not the first to try and get in this place. Check that guy out!"

"So we're not the first to find this place," Selena said coolly. "But judging by the state of these bones it looks we might be the first in a *very* long time."

Diana looked nervously at the skeleton and chewed her lip. "What killed him?"

Acosta said, "There's no sign of any bone damage. No broken skull or evidence of any hacking or stab wounds. I'd say poison, maybe from a dart."

"Then we have to be careful." Decker scanned the surrounding area for anywhere likely to contain hidden blowpipes. "The good news is we haven't set anything off yet."

"Yet," Charlie said. "Which isn't that reassuring when you stop to think about it."

Riley was also looking into the trees. "Not necessarily a fixed weapon though. Might have been fired from a mobile pipe by a warrior or someone charged with protecting this place."

"You think that person might still be alive?" Diana asked.

"Not unless he's five hundred years old," Selena said, staring at the skeleton. "So let's just pull ourselves together and get on with it. It'll be night soon and we need to get going. Now, get those bones out the way, and let me get into the burial chamber!"

"That's my girl," Atticus said proudly. "Never lets anything get in her way. Not even a skeleton."

As she elbowed past him, Decker gave her a doubtful glance. "I like a woman with ambition, but this is ridiculous. Have you no respect for the dead?"

"I'm an archaeologist, Mitch! I spend most of my life around very dead people!"

He shrugged. "When you put it like that..."

Selena turned the handle, pushed open the door, and led the way inside the passageway. She went carefully, raising her flashlight and illuminating the damp, stony interior. Angling the beam upwards, she saw the tunnel's ceiling had been reinforced with broad slabs of rocks.

"Doesn't look too safe, but if it's been holding the place together for the last five hundred years, I guess nothing's going to change today."

"I hope you're right," Decker said, joining her inside the tunnel and sweeping his own flashlight across the rock ceiling. "Looks like sandstone. Each of those rocks must weigh at least a thousand pounds. If one of them comes down on any of us, it's Goodnight Vienna."

"We can talk about this later," Charlie said. "I think the armed thugs just turned up!"

Decker's shoulders sloped and he sighed. "Are you kidding me?"

Charlie was at the back of the line, still outside with Diana and Acosta. He turned and looked off to his right, ducking down a little to keep his head down. "No jokes. Several men, all heavily armed."

"They must have parked out of sight," Selena said.

Decker said, "They were *waiting* for us to show them the way inside, damn it!"

"But how could they know?" Atticus asked.

"Don't ask me difficult questions at this time of the day," Decker growled. "Never do that."

"Oh, bugger!" Charlie said. "I think they saw me!"

Then the firing started – tracer bullets zipped through the gathering tropical dusk and pinged off the stonework around the entrance.

"Everyone get in here!" Decker yelled. "Now!"

"We don't even know where it leads!" Diana said.

"It's our only chance," Decker said. "And I know where those bullets lead!"

Atticus nodded. "I agree. We must have faith in Montesino, Diana. If he says there is a hidden site here, then there must be. He also said there were two entrances to the burial chamber, remember? When we get inside we can find what we need and use the other one to get away."

"That's a plan, then!" Decker said, rolling his eyes. "Maybe we could stop talking now?"

Riley drew his Browning Hi-Power from his holster. Charlie's weapon was a Glock, which he now drew and gripped confidently in his hand. "You guys go on ahead and find the chamber," the Australian said. "Me and Charlie will keep these pricks out of your hair for a bit."

Decker and Selena looked at one another, each already knowing what the other was thinking.

"Fine," she said at last. "But don't do anything stupid like getting yourselves killed!"

"I'm not planning on it!" Riley said. "What about you, Charlie?"

"Not today, no."

Riley caught sight of some movement outside the passageway and turned to see a man crouch-walking down the path they had cleared, slowly closing on their position. He was carrying what looked like an M249 light machine gun. Riley leveled his gun and took a shot at him, ripping a bullet into his thigh and sending him crashing to the jungle floor, shrieking and screaming and clutching at his wrecked leg.

He turned back to the others. "What are you waiting for, losers? Get on with it! Get to the chamber!"

The crew looked to Decker, and he gave a casual shrug. "I guess the guy can shoot straight enough to keep us safe. Let's go!"

10

Decker was in the lead now, pounding down the tunnel with his flashlight gripped in his hand and desperately praying there really was a way through at the other end of the chamber. Riley and Charlie were still at the entrance, returning fire on the attackers as Selena, Diana, Atticus, and Acosta followed the American into the gloom.

"You find anything down there, Mitch?" Riley shouted. He took another shot and watched the thugs scatter behind tropical undergrowth running with rainwater. "Because we're outnumbered up here! They're everywhere and all armed to the teeth."

"Yeah... I'm working on it, Riley!" he yelled back.

Decker heard the Australian let loose another shot while Charlie reloaded. "How many mags you got, mate?"

"This is the last one," Charlie said. "You?"

"Same here."

Their conversation faded out as Decker sprinted further down the passageway.

"I hope they're okay," Diana said.

"They'll be fine," said Decker. "They're both ex-soldiers and they know how to handle a solid defensive position like that entrance back there. Their only problem is if they get too outgunned, in which case they'll just retreat and join us back here."

"I pray you're right."

"He is!"

Riley's voice. Still running along the tunnel, Decker glanced over his shoulder and saw the Australian and

Charlie sprinting up behind them.

"How many?" Decker asked.

"Too many to count, and they're on their way down here. Just seconds behind us."

"Holy crap! We haven't even reached the chamber yet!"

Hearing the men gaining on them, Charlie spun around and unleashed several rounds down the tunnel. The muzzle flashed in the darkness and illuminated the men's faces. He hit one in the chest and he tumbled over into the dirt. Then his associates returned fire.

"Shit, we're in deep!" Riley called out. He raised his Hi-Power and fired into the black, the sound of his weapon almost deafeningly loud in the enclosed tunnel. "We need to get out of this passageway right now, or we're Swiss cheese, Mitch!"

Decker ignored the imagery. He knew they were massively outnumbered and if they didn't reach the chamber soon, they would be caught in a dead-end. The phrase 'shooting fish in a barrel' wouldn't do the situation justice if these men hunted them down inside the tunnel. But the darkest hour was just before dawn, and then he saw it. Up ahead, the dim outline of a stone door inside an archway made of a smooth stone plinth resting on two vertical stacks of carved rock.

"We made it!" he called out from the front. "I see some kind of door up ahead."

The crew followed him down the last remaining few yards of the tunnel until they reached a large stone archway.

"We're here!" Selena said. "That's the good news."

"What's the bad news?" Diana asked.

"*Here* is just an antechamber. The main event is behind that!" She pointed to the stone slab blocking the entrance.

"At least we're in the right place," Decker said.

"Yeah," said Charlie, "but those psychos are also going to be in the right place in about thirty seconds!"

"How do we get it open?" Riley said, glancing over his shoulder. "Right now we're just rats in a trap!"

Selena swept her flashlight over the door. Everywhere she looked, she saw carvings of dots, dashes, and what looked like tiny seashells. "Um… let me see. I wonder what these mean?"

"Wonder faster than that, Lena," Riley said.

"They're maths symbols," Atticus said. "Remember the Maya counting system?"

"Um…"

"And look closer darling," he said with a mischievous grin. "What do you see?"

Selena gasped. "Of course! I see it now. This slab is locking the way into the main chamber and maths is the key!"

"Math," Decker said.

"Not now, Mitchell," Selena said in clipped tones. "I'm thinking." She tapped her lip and cocked her head to one side, deep in thought. "Shells, dots, dashes. It's the ancient Maya script, both words, and numerals. Seems to be some sort of puzzle."

"Remember, it's not decimal," Atticus said. "The Maya system was like many of the older counting systems and was base-20."

"Base-20?" Charlie said.

Atticus smiled. "Vigesimal."

"Eh?"

"Based on twenty," Selena said. "It's not hard, Charles."

"Oh, sure."

"It's a superior system, in my opinion," Atticus said dreamily. "After all, twenty is divisible by more numbers than ten. But then, I'm old-fashioned."

"And crazy!" Riley said, turning and firing on the men and driving them back once more. "Do you even remember we're being hunted by armed maniacs?"

A bullet ripped between them and ricocheted off the top of the stone plinth above the slab.

"Damn it!" Decker cried out, moving away from the slab and joining Riley and Charlie at the rear. "We have to hold them back!"

He fired and drove the men back again. Riley and Charlie also opened fire and forced the invaders further back around the bend in the tunnel.

"We can't keep them away forever," Riley said. "Only until the bullets run out."

"We need more progress, Dad," Selena said with a sigh.

Atticus frowned as he studied the carvings. "The shell is worth zero, right?"

She nodded. "Yes, and then it's a various combination of dots and dashes to create any number you like. It's asking us a question though, right here." She leaned closer and studied the Maya script carefully. "It says two sons and two fathers went hunting together. They killed precisely three curassows. Then each hunter had one curassow."

"What the hell does that mean?" Riley called over.

Charlie said, "And what's a curassow?"

"It's a type of bird," Atticus said haughtily. "It was hunted for food in ancient Maya culture."

"But it doesn't even make sense," said Decker. "Two sons and two fathers went hunting. They killed three of these birds. Three. Then it says they had one each, which is four. Does not make sense."

"That's why they call it a riddle," Acosta said. "Perhaps they should have just left a key under the doormat so men like those shooting us could just walk in whenever they felt like it?"

"Your attitude is affecting my aim, *Pepe*," Decker said, taking another shot.

"The answer is one of the fathers was also a grandfather," Selena said. "It's an old maths riddle. One man was both the father of his son and the grandfather of his grandson. Three men."

Decker smiled. "Not bad work, Professor Moore."

"Why thank you, Captain Decker!" she said.

Riley grinned. "She's not just a pretty face."

"Indeed not, gentlemen," Selena said. "So now I simply push the tiles for grandfather, son, and grandson in that precise order and just like that..."

A large puff of dust burst out of the gap at the sides and top of the slab and a deep grinding noise filled the antechamber. Seconds later, the slab had retracted behind the stone wall and given way onto a darker inner chamber. Waving a thick cloud of dust away from her face, Selena turned and gave the team a triumphant smile. "I thank you!"

They rushed inside the chamber. "I'll thank you later," Decker said. "For now, can we close this door again?"

"I don't see why not," Selena said. "It opened easily enough, but not sure how."

"I see how," said Decker, angling a flashlight beam at the wall encasing the slab. "There's a system of ropes and pullies here. It operates a fairly simple counterweight rig. When you pushed the tiles in the correct order it was a bit like a tumbler lock letting the rope slide down and in turn pulling the door on these rollers. From this side, we can just put our shoulders against the end of it and push it right back over. There's no way they can get the necessary purchase to open it again from the other side."

Diana frowned. "That means we're safe, right?"

"Sure..."

The flashlights carried by the armed men bobbed into sight as they regained their courage and turned the final bend in the tunnel. One of them shouted in Spanish and then their weapons lit up the darkness once again.

Riley and Charlie tucked in behind the stone archway and returned fire as Decker, Acosta, and Selena pushed the heavy stone slab along the rollers and closed the doorway back up.

"That was too close for comfort!" Diana said.

"And here they come!" said Selena. "I can hear them outside."

They heard the men approach the entrance, screaming and shouting in Spanish. Someone was kicking the stone door, another pounding on it with his fists. Then another opened fire on it. They all heard the pointless shots ricochet off into the tunnel behind them.

"Not a chance," Decker said. "This slab weighs way too much. No way are they shooting through it."

"Are you sure?" Diana asked. "If they get in, we're dead."

"Don't count on it," Riley said. "I'm not going down without one hell of a fight."

"Me neither," said Charlie.

"The only way they're getting through that door is if one of them knows how to read Maya script, understands the ancient counting system, and can work out the riddle," Selena said. "Which is highly unlikely, given what a bunch of monkeys they looked like back in the jungle."

"We can't be certain though," Atticus said. "We should press on while we have an advantage."

And with that, they turned their flashlights into the pitch-black of the main burial chamber and started searching for Montesino's mysterious doomsday machine.

They didn't have to look for very long.

11

"Over there!" Atticus said. "On the altar."

He shone his flashlight on a carved stone slab and walked closer toward it, his heart full of anticipation. Then, his hopes were dashed. The altar was empty and there was no sign of either the priest's grave or Montesino's strange device. Carved into the wall behind it, a giant bas-relief of Huracan stood silent sentinel over the chamber.

"Gosh!" Selena said, looking at the carvings on the altar. "This is odd."

"Just what I was thinking," said Atticus.

The rest of the crew joined them around the massive stone slab. "What's odd about it?" Decker asked.

"First, there's no sign of anything Montesino wrote about. Second, these carvings seem to be describing the infamous snake kings of the Kaanul Dynasty."

"And this is odd, why?" asked the American.

"Because the Kaanul Dynasty was based quite far north from here, in an area roughly comprised of Mexico's Campeche state and northern Guatemala, not here in this part of Belize."

Riley was frowning. "Wait, what the hell was that about snake kings?"

"They weren't actually snakes, Riley," Selena said with an eye roll. "Do try and be sensible."

"Sure, but when someone says snake kings in a place like this, your imagination tends to start whirring."

She frowned. "Well, just relax. The snake kings were just normal men who idolized snakes. The worship of reptiles and snakes was all too common around the ancient world. No one knows exactly why."

"So it's definitely *not* because humanity was seeded on the Earth millions of years ago by a race of hyper-intelligent interdimensional reptilian overlords who still to this day rule over us?"

"Riley?"

"What?"

She put her hands on her hips and fixed her eyes on him. "We're back to you having to shut up again, aren't we?"

"Is that a 'no' on the lizard kings, then?"

"It is a *solid* no on the time-traveling lizard kings or whatever drivel you just spouted. As I just said, and I think both patiently and with great aplomb – many ancient cultures worshipped reptiles and snakes. The tombs at Holmul that I mentioned earlier back in the Jeep also contained a strange pendant devoted to the sun-god which we think offers a clue about these mysterious snake kings."

"And they're absolutely not real snakes?" Riley asked with a grin.

"I thought we established you had to be quiet now?"

He made a gesture pretending to zip up his lips and took a step back.

Selena said, "The ruling family who we call the snake kings are called that because they used a very unique snakehead as their dynasty's emblem."

"But why did they choose that particular emblem?" Charlie asked.

Riley hissed. "Because they were half-reptilian, mate!"

"Oh, do stop being such a tit," Selena said.

"Hey!"

"I can't answer that specifically, Charlie," she said.

"Different families used different creatures from the natural world to represent them. More interesting is that one of the jade pieces – a beautiful piece, half cormorant and half sun-god, bore the name of one of these snake kings, even though his dynasty ruled an area hundreds of miles away."

"So what?" Riley asked.

Acosta gasped. "Such ignorance! This finding tells us so much about the ancient Maya kingdoms! The extent of their political and diplomatic influence, where they traded... the list goes on."

Riley shrugged. "Just a question, mate."

Acosta shook his head and mumbled in Spanish.

Then, Atticus spoke. "Look over here, Lena! Look at the colors! This azul maya is as fresh as the day it was painted."

"Azul maya?" Charlie asked.

"Maya blue," Atticus said. "It's a very unique pigment made by the ancient Maya. And unless I'm very much mistaken, these are references to the same divine power, the same Stormbringer that Montesino wrote about."

Selena stepped away from Riley and Charlie and walked over to her father. Raising her flashlight beam to add more light to his, she gasped when she saw the glyphs he had been studying.

"My God! You're right."

"What does it say?" Decker asked.

She ran her hand over the intricately carved glyphs on the stone wall behind the altar. "Um, let me think. It starts with a warning, telling anyone searching for the power to give up and turn back before it's too late." She blew some dust away from the bas-relief carvings. "And these glyphs here say whosoever shall persist with the hunt will be wrenched asunder by the mighty power of the gods."

"Excellent," Riley said. "I don't know about you guys,

but that is *just* what I wanted to hear today."

"What is *asunder*?" Diana asked. "I am not sure I know the meaning of this word."

"It's archaic," Atticus said. "And sometimes literary, so I'm not surprised you don't know it, my dear. It means *apart*."

"So they are saying…"

Charlie sighed. "That if we don't pack up our little backpacks and fly away with our tails between our legs, the gods are going to rip us into pieces."

"But whatever can that mean?" Diana asked. "Ripped apart by what?"

Selena tapped the stone wall. "By the Power of the Gods, I suppose. The Stormbringer. Exactly what that means, I don't know. They don't elaborate here, and Montesino was also strangely reluctant to describe it."

"Maybe he was too terrified," Acosta whispered. "Too scared even to write down what he had seen in any further detail than he managed in the Codex. This is what I think. Whatever he witnessed all those centuries ago struck such a terrible fear into his heart, he could not bring himself to detail it in the Codex beyond a few simple sentences. This is my belief."

"It's as good a theory as any other we have," Atticus said. "That's for sure."

"These glyphs here say the power must not be removed from the altar," Selena said.

Charlie shone his flashlight on the flat, smooth altar stone. "Unless we're talking about the power of invisibility, I'd say it's a little late for that."

Decker stepped into the light. "Excuse me for being dumb enough to ask the obvious question, but if this power is so goddam awesome, shouldn't we at least be able to *see* what it is? I mean, look at this place! It's empty! Totally empty. We're exactly where Montesino told us to come in the Codex and yet there's nothing here except a bare stone altar and a warning carved into a wall. C'mon…"

"C'mon what?" Selena asked. "You're not suggesting he made it all up?"

"Right now, all I know is we're in danger. Don't forget about the guys who just tried to blow our heads off! They're still out there."

"And we're still in here," Diana said. "Without a clue to the location of this divine power."

"But that's not true," Atticus said. "We *do* have a clue."

12

Selena turned to him. "Would you care to repeat that, father?"

A broad smile appeared on his face. "The last line of glyphs here has been added at a later date, don't you think?"

She studied the carvings he was pointing out. "I suppose it's possible."

"It's more than possible, Lena! These last few glyphs were added by a totally different stonemason, and they seem to offer us some sort of indication about what happened to the Stormbringer."

"What is it?"

"Some sort of map, and it says the Underworld holds the key!"

Atticus lowered himself to his knees and started brushing sand and dust away from the tiles to reveal a large stone seal carved into the floor. Perfectly circular, the seal was around twenty inches across and carved from pure jade. When they had removed all the sand and made the entire carving visible, they saw it was sitting at the heart of a complex image carved into the floor tiles, stretching all the way to the wall behind the altar.

"But it's just gibberish," Selena said. "Read it again! The glyphs make no sense at all, Dad."

"Are you sure about that?" he said with a devilish smile on his face.

She turned and stared at them again, frustration obviously rising inside her. "All right, I give up."

"That's no good!" Atticus said. "Unless you're giving

up-side-down!"

Her mouth fell open a little. "Ha! The glyphs are upside down!"

"And back to front. Now, try again."

"My goodness!" she said. "This is brilliant! Amazing! Enlightening!" She stopped and stared at her father, paling. "Terrifying!"

The faces of the rest of the crew froze.

"Why that last one?" Charlie said. "I was okay with brilliant and amazing and enlightening. I really liked enlightening. But not terrifying."

"I agree," said Diana. "What is so terrifying?"

Selena and Atticus fell silent, each taking another look at the glyphs. Acosta pushed forward through the small crew for a closer look.

"I'm no specialist in ancient Mayan glyphs," he said, squinting. "But I agree. This does not look good."

Riley sighed. "Would one of the eggheads in this room…"

"Hidden chamber," Selena corrected him. "We're in a hidden chamber, not a room."

"Fine. Would one of the eggheads in this *hidden chamber* please tell the rest of us just what the hell is going on? Even I'm starting to get worried and I'm as hard as a six-inch tungsten nail!"

"And so modest," Selena purred.

He shrugged. "You know me, Lena."

"Yes," she said, sighing. "Unfortunately, I do. Anyway, the good news is, we know why Montesino's divine power is not here."

"Why?" Decker asked.

"It was moved."

"Whoa," Charlie said. "This logic is getting too complex for me. It's not here because it was *moved*? I can't follow this."

"All right, Charles," Atticus said. "There's no need for your particular brand of impertinence. What my daughter is trying to say is that the Stormbringer is real, it exists, and that it was moved by a Maya priest after one of the snake kings tried to seize it for use in battle."

"It says that?" Diana asked.

He nodded. "Clearly. It says here that the power of Huracan was removed to stop an insane snake king from trying to find it and abuse it."

"Fair enough," Riley said.

"And see here," Selena said. "These glyphs are not only upside down and back to front, presumably to stop casual thieves, looters, *and* ignorant, barbaric snake kings from finding the new location. They are also presented in obscure riddle form. However, I believe between my father and me, we have formed a good translation and should be able to discern the new location of the power. Starting here – this glyph here is a ceiba tree."

Charlie frowned. "Doesn't look like a tree."

"Upside down, remember?" Selena said. "The ceiba tree is very special in ancient Maya culture. They believed the world was split into three basic levels – the heavens, the earth, and the underworld. According to their religion, the ceiba tree grew through all three realms, with the roots starting in the underworld, the trunk coming up through the earth – this plane we are now standing on – and the canopy opening up in the heavens."

"Fascinating," Riley said. "Where's the gold?"

Atticus gave him a look and took over. "The ancient Maya also believed that the world was constituted of what they called the four cardinal directions – east, west, north, and south. The heart of all these, or the center, was where the ceiba tree grew. East was the most important because of the rising sun."

Selena crouched down and ran her fingers over the

carved ridges. "This glyph here appears to be Huracan, the god of storms. I'm guessing these lines represent his power. As you can all see, the image of Huracan is located in the roots of the ceiba tree."

"In the underworld?" Diana said.

Selena nodded. "Exactly."

"Great," Decker said. "We're going to hell. Anyone have a handbasket we can travel in?"

"Funny." Charlie chuckled, turning to leave. "I hope you guys find what you're looking for in hell. Send me a postcard if... I mean *when* you make it!"

"You're going nowhere, Valentine," Selena said. "Get your backside back here!"

"But I just want to drink banana daiquiris on Kantiang Beach! I don't want to go to hell in a handbasket and find the power of the gods!"

"Then you signed up to the wrong crew," Decker said. "Because that's exactly what we're going to do!"

"And not just anywhere in hell," Atticus said grimly. "We're going to the ninth level of hell!"

"Huh?" Decker said, suddenly less confident.

Selena got to her feet and brushed her clothes down. "The ancient Maya believed the underworld was made up of nine levels of hell. You can see this represented in their temples which very often have nine levels, Chichen Itza being the most famous example."

"So we really are going to burn in hell!" Charlie said. "Imagine the endless, horrendous baking misery of all that heat and fire."

"Sounds like February back on the station," Riley said wistfully. "Damn, I really miss that place."

"Sorry to disappoint you," Atticus said. "But what you have just described is a Western or Christian conception of hell. To the ancient Maya, hell is not about the fire at all, but a cold, dark and dank realm."

"What, like England?" Riley said.

Selena scowled at him. "I'm going to pretend I didn't hear that, Corporal Carr."

"Probably just as well," said the Australian.

"Anyway," Selena said. "Getting back to business, the Maya saw hell as a cold and dark place because it was down in the roots of the ceiba tree. And Maya mythology is all about people struggling with the gods of the underworld and creation and destruction. It's a busy realm."

"And now we're going there to find the source of Huracan's power..." Diana's words trailed away into the gloom.

"But where is *there*?" Decker asked.

"That's easy enough," Atticus said. "This part of the seal over here is a map and it seems to indicate where we can find the specific entrance to Xibalba."

"And what is Xibalba?" Riley asked.

"The place of fright," Atticus said. "It's just the Mayan word for their underworld."

"There's that word *hell* again!" said Charlie.

"You might say that, but it's not an exact translation."

"So no demons then..." Diana said. "Thank God."

"Well, there's always the Camazotz..." Atticus mumbled.

Selena looked at him sharply. "Don't tell them that!"

"Don't tell them what?" said Decker.

Selena sighed. "The Camazotz were monsters found in Xibalba. The word means death bat."

Riley slapped his hands together. "Excellent news! I've always wanted to fight death bats. Throw in some lizard kings and I've nearly got something to write home about!"

"Maybe we could get back to reality for a second," Decker said. "Where is the entrance to this Xibalba place?"

Atticus said, "According to this, it's in a cave inside Flower Mountain."

"Flower Mountain?" asked Diana.

"It's a sort of Maya paradise," Acosta said. "I thought it was mythical... that it didn't really exist, until now."

"Where is this place?" Decker asked.

Atticus squinted at the map. "If my understanding is right, then I would say north of Lake Miramar."

"And where might that be?" Charlie asked.

"It's in the Lacandon Jungle," said the old English professor. "One of the most untouched areas of Middle America. Talk about the middle of nowhere!"

"Then we'd better get moving," Decker said. "Someone get a picture of that damned seal."

Charlie leaned forward and snapped a picture with his phone. "All done."

"Then it's time to go," Selena said.

"I don't think so!"

The voice shattered the silent darkness, a cold, hard voice with a rich Yucatan Spanish accent.

"What the hell?" Decker said.

The armed men rushed into the far end of the chamber with their guns raised. As their shadows bobbed about in the gloom, Decker reached for his weapon. "Are we all ready for some CQB?"

"For what?" Diana asked.

"Close quarter battle," he said with a shrug.

"It won't come to that, surely!" she said.

Before he could answer, the men opened fire on them.

13

Bullets traced through the chamber's dusty air, forcing the team to drop to the floor and find somewhere safe out of the line of fire. As the team scattered, Diana scrambled behind the altar and tucked up in a ball at the base of the stone sculpture of Huracan, cradling her head in her arms and holding her breath.

Not for the first time, the gunfire frightened her so much she felt like crying. Unlike the rest of her friends in the Avalon crew, except for Selena, her background was not military or secret service. She led the simple and safe existence of an academic in her homeland of Portugal. As a specialist in ancient languages and paleography, she had looked forward to a stable and rewarding life in the academy, but then her old friend Selena Moore had called her up and asked her to help find the mythical Tibetan kingdom of Shambhala.

After that, everything changed.

A bullet struck the pillar at the head of the Huracan statue, ricocheting inches from her head and spraying her with stone fragments. She screamed and tucked herself even tighter into a ball, suddenly overwhelmed with the fear she was about to get shot. What would it feel like? She imagined a red hot piece of lead tearing through her body and shuddered at the thought. She didn't know how the rest of the crew felt about it, but she wasn't about to get used to getting shot any time soon.

"You okay, Di?"

Riley's voice. She peeked through her arms and saw the young Australian firing a burst of rounds from a nasty-looking handgun. He was scrambling over to her through the dust. The noise of his gun was deafeningly loud, not to mention all the smoke and the smell of ignited gunpowder. It made her feel sick.

"I'm okay, thanks."

He was next to her now. "Keep your head down, mate. I mean it."

The former SASR corporal was a kidder with all his jokes and gags, but in business hours he was the most serious man she had ever known. With a look of stern concentration on his lean, tanned face and the gun cradled in the classic two-handed hold, Riley Carr twisted his upper body and fired another peal of rounds into the head of a man trying to run toward them.

With each shot, Diana jumped, but this time kept the impulse to scream in check. The killing business was violent and bloody. A man shot in the head was not a good thing to see or hear, and these were sights and sounds she could live without. Skulls did not break apart easily, and watching brain matter spraying over a stone wall was something you never forgot.

She hated it.

The attackers took cover but kept fighting with the intensity of men who were days away from the discovery of their lifetimes, and the unlimited wealth and power that would come with it. She guessed these were hardened criminals and thugs, but they were not stupid men, nor were they cowards. Like the rest of the crew, she knew they would fight to the death to beat them to Montesino's ancient secret and the doomsday device he had described in his Codex.

She was suddenly aware of Decker's voice. The American was closer to the entrance, firing on other men and now diving for cover behind what looked like a boulder. It was hard to see in the smoke, and chaos now reigned supreme in the chamber. Then, the men charged toward them once again and began fighting in an even greater explosion of rage.

Riley aimed and fired but his weapon was out of rounds. He wasted no time. No curses, no complaints. He tossed the gun to the floor and snatched at a hand shovel in one of their packs at his feet. He weighed it in his hands and then spun it across the chamber at the men running toward them. The cutting edge of the dusty sheet steel blade gouged a rugged gash in one of their throats. He was dead before he hit the floor.

At the same moment, Charlie made a running jump to the altar and used its smooth stone surface to launch himself at the rest of the men as they fanned out into the chamber. Atticus and Acosta were sheltering in an alcove with Selena, each looking more terrified than she had ever seen them before. Selena made a break for Decker but one of the men caught up with her.

"Wait here!" Riley said.

He got to his feet just in time to see Selena delivering a brutal kick right into the center of the man's face. After the strike, she rotated around one-eighty degrees, bringing her foot back down to the floor and putting her hands on her hips. "Nicely done, even if I do say so my—"

Her words were cut short when one of the other bandits hurled himself at her and tackled her to the floor. She hit the flagstones with a hefty thump and cried out in pain, alerting Decker to what had just happened. He turned to see her struggling with the man and called out to her.

"Are you okay?"

"Never... better..."

A man with a long black ponytail rushed Decker and shoulder-barged him to the floor. He threw a punch and Decker dodged it. The American forced him back with his knees but the two men were quickly embroiled in a brutal fist fight and Selena was still fighting for her life.

"I'm on my way!" Riley yelled, still running across the chamber under a hail of bullets.

Charlie watched him from across the chamber. "You're one crazy, jacked-up, adrenaline-pumped, maverick, Riley!"

"I am not crazy!" Riley yelled back. "I'll give you a pass on the rest."

Decker delivered a savage uppercut to his opponent's face, smashing the man's jaw shut and knocking him out on the spot before rushing over and grabbing hold of the man attacking Selena.

"You took your sweet time," she said between breaths.

Riley arrived at the same time. "Sorry, I'm late!"

"Job's taken, Riley," Decker said.

With a chunky fistful of the sweat-streaked flannel shirt in his hands, the former US Marine heaved the heavy man away from Selena and pulled him to his feet. He recoiled his fist and aimed it in the center of his face. "Son…of…a…"

Smack!

The punch spread the man's nose all over his face and sent him tumbling backward into Selena. She was still trying to get to her feet, and now the man tripped over her body and fell back onto the flagstones.

Decker padded over to him, ready to finish the job, but Selena was now back up and running and stopped him. "Please, allow me."

"You think you can handle it?"

As the man crawled up to his hands and knees, blood pouring from his splattered nose, Selena shut one eye and aimed squarely between his legs. After a short run-up to gather some forward momentum, she planted her right boot right where it counted most. The man's squeals filled the chamber but were silenced when she ran around to his head, lifted it from the floor, and cracked it back down again on the hard tiles.

"There," she said, dusting her hands off. "You can count him out for the rest of the day's play."

Decker looked at the man with something approaching pity. "I guess you *could* handle him."

She walked past him and winked. "You betcha, Mitch."

"Why is it so quiet in here?" said Riley. "I was just getting warmed up!"

"Because the fight is over," Atticus said, his voice thin in the smoky darkness.

"What do you mean?" Selena asked.

"I mean the other men have gone." His voice grew dark. "And they took the jade seal with them. They have the map of Flower Mountain with them."

Decker ached and rubbed his jaw where one of the men had punched him. "Ain't that just fantastic."

"So, what now?" Diana asked.

"It's obvious," Selena said. "As of this moment, we are officially in a race with those thugs to find Flower Mountain and secure the Stormbringer."

"And we're going to need to know who we're up against," Charlie said. "I can help with that. I have a lot of good friends in the intel community. Let me make some calls when we're back on the surface."

"All right," Decker said. "Let's go back to the plane."

14

They reached Maya Flats after sunset and walked across the airfield in silence. Above their heads, a rich Egyptian blue canvas littered with tropical stars stretched down to the horizon, but none of them saw it. Each of the crew members made their way over to the shining silver hull of the Avalon with a heavy heart, their heads roiling with the gunfight back at the ruins.

Climbing up inside the aircraft, they each slumped down on a seat and did whatever they could to get their heads together. After a few seconds, Charlie's phone bleeped and alerted him to an incoming message. He opened it and read it. Then, with everyone sitting and watching him with bated breath, he told them what his old friend at MI5 had just sent him.

"The good news first," he began. "Thanks to the security camera here at the airfield, my contacts in MI5 managed to get an ID on some of the men who attacked us at the ruins."

"Great!" Selena said. "Who are they?"

"That's the bad news," he said with a frown. "First, the boss is a man named Ramon Morales. Originally from Acapulco, he now lives in Cancún. He goes by the moniker Tarántula, earned because of his obsession with the spider. Runs one of the biggest drugs cartels in Mexico and trails a body-count as long as a freight train behind him."

"Sounds nasty."

"And he doesn't work alone. His bodyguard is a serious criminal named Diego Novarro – he was the guy with the ponytail and tattoos. Others in his gang are Carlos and Miguel Mercado, two brothers from Mexico City heavily involved in the smuggling trade. In their case, that means mostly class A narcotics, but they're not fussy. They use their black market contacts and criminal network to smuggle anything into anywhere."

"Cripes," Riley said. "They sound like real meanies."

"They are," Charlie continued. "They're known to MI5 because of the part they played in a smuggling ring bringing Mexican cocaine into the United Kingdom a few years ago. Part of the original shipment went to Southampton and part went into Miami. The American authorities got a tip-off and caught them in the act and they were sentenced to life behind bars in Colorado."

"Life?" Diana said. "For drug smuggling?"

"First, it was a *lot* of drugs, tens of millions of dollars in street value. Enough to keep Florida high for the next decade. Second, both men were on the FBI's Most Wanted List for gangland murders within the United States. Carlos, the older brother, shot a man in…"

"Reno?" Riley said.

Selena slapped his shoulder. "Silence!"

"Sorry."

"Not Reno," Charlie said. "But it was in Nevada. He killed a man outside a casino in Vegas."

"And the younger brother?" Atticus asked.

"Miguel," said Charlie. "He stabbed a man to death in El Paso outside a nightclub. In both cases, they used their smuggling network to get out of the country undetected and since the US-Mexican extradition treaty doesn't include citizens of their own countries, the Mexican authorities refused to send them over the Rio Grande."

"But they went into Florida," Acosta said. "You already said they were busted there."

"Under false names," Charlie said. "In fact, during the

trial, the US authorities found out both men had properties in Florida and regularly traveled there, usually entering illegally on boats used by their own smuggling networks. My contact tells me they are both extremely dangerous men with volatile tempers. Carlos, especially, is well-known for being unpredictable and extremely unforgiving toward his enemies. Less than a year after the trial, the head of the man who tipped off the FBI about the Miami drugs operation was found in a garbage can outside a police station in Tampa."

"Que nojento!" Diana muttered, turning her head in disgust.

Riley nodded. "If that means *holy crap*, then at least I don't have to say it, too."

"It's close enough," she said.

"Anything else on Tarántula?" Decker asked. "Specifically, why the sudden interest in archaeological relics and doomsday machines? Is he planning something?"

Charlie shook his head. "Rich has nothing on that. Sorry."

"Nothing to be sorry about, old man," Atticus said, giving him a hearty pat on the back. "Your friend has done a wonderful job. Now we know who we're up against."

"And it's not good," Acosta said. "These men sound like animals. I mean, to order someone's decapitation like that..."

"I hear that," Riley said. "Sounds like they're both off their heads."

"I'm not even going to comment on that remark," Selena said.

Riley grinned. "But didn't you just do exactly that?"

"And didn't I just tell you to be silent?"

He put his arm around her and squeezed her. "You'd

miss me if I wasn't here."

"I wouldn't miss," Selena said. "I'd aim straight for between the eyes."

"Funny."

Decker frowned. "Maybe this Tarántula just found out Montesino was on the trail of something else, something valuable – I mean seriously financially valuable like gems or gold or something and they want it for themselves, or maybe even to smuggle for someone else. Maybe they don't know anything about the doomsday machine."

Atticus sighed. "Consider this. Apart from the rumors spread by the idiot Danvers, the only real evidence of the Stormbringer is inside the Codex, which only we have read. With this in mind, I think we have to presume something like Mitch has just suggested," he said glumly. "Just our luck, too! We finally get the Codex and discover the Stormbringer is probably real and we find ourselves up against a bunch of murderous cartel thugs out for loot."

"Then we just have to be extra vigilant on this mission, Dad," Selena said. "We can do that."

"Did your contact get an ID on any of the other men who attacked us?" Acosta asked.

Charlie looked down at his phone and began scrolling through his old friend's message. "Only one of them. The one with the face tattoos and the red bandana is called Diablo."

"His parents called him the Devil?" Diana asked with wide eyes.

"No, it's just a gang name. They don't know his real name. Very little is known about him except he's not part of Tarántula's normal smuggling network. He's a sort of freelance thug and killer who works for the highest bidder. Some say he was the guy who took off the grass's head and threw it in the dumpster behind the police station in Tampa."

"Well, isn't that just the best news?" Diana said. "I'm so glad I decided to come along on this mission."

"Take it easy, mate," Riley said, suddenly all business. "Anyone wants to hurt you, they're coming through me first."

"Thanks, Riley," she said, reaching out and squeezing his arm. "That actually makes me feel much better."

"No worries."

"All right. Let's get going," Decker said, getting up from the seat and heading up to the cockpit. "The sooner we start, the sooner we get out to Lake Miramar. Thanks to the Avalon being a flying boat, I can set her down right in the middle of the lake. That should save us the time of having to find the nearest airfield and driving all the way out there, at least."

*

An hour later, the old Grumman Albatross was sailing high over the Yucatan Peninsula. They were at eighteen thousand feet now and flying towards the west and the North Pacific Ocean. Decker eased back into the worn leather seat and breathed out a low sigh. Nothing like cruising above a tropical paradise in your own plane, he thought.

This was the life he loved, but it was time for a change. Back in Mexico City a few days ago, he had wandered into a jewelry store and paid a fair sum of money for a beautiful emerald and diamond engagement ring. He'd first had the feeling he wanted to get hitched to Selena way back on their first mission to Shambhala and it had gotten worse from there. Maybe now was the time to ask.

Maybe not.

What if she said no? Feisty didn't begin to describe Professor Selena Moore. It was just possible her answer might cause irreparable damage to his ego. Maybe it would be better if he just forgot all about it and took the ring back. That sounded like the safest play.

After another quick scan of the instrument panel, he peered outside and gazed at the endless rainforest passing beneath them. Belize was long gone now, replaced by the breadnut and mahogany forests of Guatemala's Maya Biosphere Reserve. This was a full fifth of the small country and over twenty thousand square kilometers.

He'd read some time ago in a National Geographic about it becoming one of UNESCO's biosphere models, a special program designed to improve the relationship between mankind and the ecosystem. He was wondering exactly what that meant when Selena walked into the cockpit and slid into the first officer's seat.

"It's a beautiful night," she said, staring out at the ribbon of violet painted across the horizon.

"Sure is."

"How long until we're at Flower Mountain?"

He glanced at the instrument panel again, checking the airspeed and then his watch. "Not long. If this tailwind keeps up, maybe less than an hour."

A few minutes of silence stretched out between them. Selena yawned and peered through the window. "It just goes on forever. You can see why we're still finding ruins and lost cities."

Decker said, "I wonder how many more surprises there are out there, still, just waiting for us to discover them."

"A lot, I would think. At least, I hope so! Without anything to discover I wouldn't have a very interesting job."

He laughed. "I guess not. I don't have to worry about that. Being a pilot always means a new challenge, a new place to fly. I'm not the type to settle down. I like life on the road, but in my case, it's a life in the air."

Selena closed her eyes and pushed back into the seat. "I wanted to talk with you about the future, Mitch."

He sat up. "Oh yeah?"

"About the future of the Avalon crew."

And slid back down again. "Oh, right."

"Actually, I have a bit of an announcement about the Avalon team's future."

"An announcement?"

"Yes, but when we're all together."

"Sounds ominous."

She paused and closed her eyes. "I do wish your aeroplane were quieter, Mitch. I can't sleep."

"I'm so sorry. Would you like me to switch the engines off for an hour so you can get some shuteye and then wake you when we're there?"

"Stop being facetious."

"C'mon! What else can I do? The damn plane needs the power to get lift, Lena. Even you know that."

"What do you mean, *even* I know it?" She opened her eyes and glared at him.

Decker reached over to the instrument panel where he had set his hat and now picked it up and wore it, pulling the brim down over the right side of his face to block her view of him. Next thing he knew, she had pulled it right off again and tossed it behind their seats.

"Hey!"

"Oh, sorry! Was that rude?"

"Yes."

"Then looks like we're even."

He hid his smile. "The lady has spirit."

"You bet I do! And I would be much happier if the pilot was actually looking at all these gauges and doing things with them instead of playing around with big hats."

"And what is wrong with my hat?"

"Well, nothing…"

From behind in the cabin, Charlie leaned his head against the seat and said, "I'm getting some sleep."

"Good idea," Selena called back. "We should all do that."

"Looks like we're late to the party," Charlie said. "Take a look."

When she turned and looked through the cockpit door down the cabin, she saw the rest of the crew were already fast asleep in their seats. Glancing back at the silhouette of Decker in the cockpit, she smiled and closed her eyes. "Get some sleep, Charlie," she said. "I'm going to keep Mitch company."

15

Lacandon Jungle, Chiapas State, Mexico

The chopper swooped over the Lacandon Jungle, so low its skids almost brushed the tops of the tropical canopies. When the Spanish conquistadors first arrived, the Lacandon tribe took one look at them and vanished inside this immense jungle. Most of them stayed hidden within it until the twentieth century arrived, but today their lands have been slashed away by logging and mining operations right across Chiapas state.

The Chiapanecan bush pilot Tarántula had hired expertly located the clearing, invisible to everyone else, and lowered the collective, bringing the helicopter down below the tree-line and gently touching down on the uneven ground. "Bienvenido a Laguna Miramar."

Tarántula unbuckled his seatbelt and stepped out of the chopper. The Snake King had already exited and was standing at the edge of the clearing, staring up at the moon. On his face, the terrifying jade mask glinted in the moonlight as he mumbled an ancient mantra to the gods.

Tarántula watched him raise his hands into the air and release a desperate, hoarse scream into the night. It echoed across the jungle and triggered a cacophony of cries from the legion of monkeys and birds within it.

"Is he all right?" Carlos said.

Tarántula turned his eyes to his old friend. "He knows what he is doing."

The heat and humidity worked together to make it feel like someone had thrown a hot, wet blanket over him. As most of the rest of his team exited the chopper, he took a breath of the hot, sticky air and wiped his forehead. "Where is the seal?"

"Here," Diablo said, hefting it from the top of his pack.

Carlos swatted a mosquito on his arm and pointed south of their position. "Which way do we go?"

Tarántula looked at the seal and mumbled. "This way, it's pointing to the north of the lake."

Novarro slung his bags over his shoulder and brushed past them. "What are we waiting for?"

Miguel took one look outside and sunk back into his seat. "I think I want to stay in the helicopter. It's so comfortable in here, and there's air-conditioning."

Tarántula adjusted his hat and blew out a deep breath. "Get out. Now."

"Do as he says, Mico," Carlos said.

"You said they have an old sea plane, right?" asked Carlos.

Diablo nodded. "This is what I am told. Why?"

"Because without a helicopter, there is nowhere to land around here for hundreds of kilometers. If they are going to land here, then they must use the lake."

Tarántula started to grin and turned to Carlos. "You hear that, old friend? Our archaeologist friends have no choice but to bring their plane down on this lake. I want you to make sure they have a welcoming committee when they arrive."

"Leave it to me, boss."

Tarántula's grin broke into a greasy smile, the diamond on his front tooth reflecting the bright moonlight. Then, the Snake King wandered back over to them, his face still concealed by the grotesque jade mask. "I am most pleased with our work here tonight. If we sacrifice the foreigners to Huracan and then locate the source of his divine power, he will greatly reward us!" He turned to the moon and fell to his knees. "Kaloomte! The king of kings!"

Tarántula and the others shared an unsettled glance as the Snake King began mumbling his prayers to Huracan.

*

The Avalon flew low with the night still at its back. As the bright Mexican moon rose rapidly above the jungle, the vintage sea plane turned to the left and swooped down toward a large lake to their southwest which had been totally invisible only moments earlier.

In the low ambient light of the cockpit, Decker turned to Selena and gently nudged her awake. "We're almost there."

"Go away and leave me alone," she mumbled. "I need at least another hour's sleep."

"Sorry, but we're about to land. Let the others know and tell them to buckle up."

Selena begrudgingly climbed out of her seat and was making her way toward the cockpit door when a loud explosion sounded in the night. A second later, the Avalon rocked wildly in the air and then lurched over to one side, sending her tumbling into Decker's lap.

"Sorry, Mitch!" she said, pulling herself up and grabbing hold of the back of his seat. "But what the hell was that?"

"I don't know, but we're going down!"

Riley's face appeared in the door. "Your flying sucks, mate! You just woke everyone up!"

"We've been hit by something," Decker called out.

"Maybe shot at. I don't know. Tell everyone to buckle up. We're going down."

"This is not what a guy wants to hear from a pilot, Mitch."

"Now, Riley!"

Riley left the cockpit and Decker scanned the instruments once again.

Only three hundred feet in the air and dropping like a stone.

He gripped the yoke with all his might and fought hard to keep the damaged aircraft in the sky. He'd been in a few scrapes in his time, but this was already the worst and it had only just begun. The enormous rotary engines, fixed on either side of the cockpit on the vintage plane's high-wing configuration, roared and whined as the Avalon's nose pitched down harder.

He glanced momentarily to his right and saw Selena. She looked scared as hell. "Listen, you'd better go back into the main cabin and strap in. Looks like we're going down hard and fast and there's nothing I can do about it except try and keep her on a track to the lake."

"And you've tried everything?" she asked, wide-eyed with fear.

"No, I thought I'd try *some* of the things I can do to stop her going down, and forget about the rest. Yes, I tried everything!"

"No need to be facetious, Mitch. I was just asking."

"I'm sorry." He swiveled in his seat and craned his neck to the left to look outside the side window one more time. "Engine seems okay but the wing surface has been badly damaged by what looks like gunfire! Bastards shot my plane to shit! Ailerons look like goddam vegetable strainers. God only knows what they did to the back, but judging from the response I'm getting up here..." he turned and fixed his eyes on her. "It ain't good."

A meaty explosion on the right. Selena jumped and swore, and then looked out of her side window. "Mitch, what would it mean if there was a thick cloud of black smoke billowing out of the back of an engine?"

Decker, who had leaned forward in his seat and was tapping the glass screen of the attitude gauge, stopped what he was doing and turned to her. "Huh?"

"Black smoke, Mitch. Pouring out of the thingy at the back of the engine."

He looked at the starboard engine's oil pressure gauge and watched the little needle slowly sinking down to zero. "Looks like they took out engine number two... sons of bitches! And it's the cowling, not a thingy."

"Perhaps rather than correcting my speech with your somewhat *niche* airman's vocabulary, you might be more concerned that the Mexican jungle is about to smash into this cockpit!"

"I think you'll find the cockpit is about to smash into the Mexican jungle, Lena."

"I swear to *God*, sometimes I could slap your—"

Riley Carr's face appeared in the cockpit door once again. "Engine two's out, Mitch, and the horizontal stabilizer on the portside looks like Swiss cheese."

"I worked that much out, but thanks."

The Australian SAS man gave a bright, toothy grin and leaned on the doorframe as casual as if he were in a beach house with a beer in his hand. "So, are we fucked or what?"

Standing behind him, Charlie didn't have to think about it. "Is Riley cool? He's straight from the fridge."

Decker was also straight from the fridge, but in his case, from the ice box. Flying planes, especially vintage aircraft, was a serious business and demanded a calm head. "I'm shutting engine number two down."

"That sounds bad," Selena said. "Is it bad?"

"It's not great, but we're okay. She can fly on one engine. I'm feathering the prop to reduce drag."

"Feathering the prop?" Riley said. "I'm an open-minded guy but please tell me that has nothing to do with a rugby player?"

Decker gave him a look. "I'm from New York state, Riley. I don't know the first thing about what happens on a rugby pitch. I'm talking about the engines."

"Phew."

"This is a variable prop aircraft, which means the propeller blades can be rotated so they're thin-side on to the wind. It reduces drag. That process is called feathering."

"Gotcha, big guy. That's a load off."

Decker rotated the blades on the dead engine and increased power to the portside one, carefully mitigating the effect with the rudder as he tried to line the aircraft up with the moonlit lake ahead of them.

Now Diana stuck her head in the cockpit door. "Are we going to be all right?"

"Sure," Decker said. "Well, everyone except Riley. There's no hope for him."

"I understand," she said. "Thanks. I'll tell the others… especially about Riley."

With the aircraft lined up, Decker pulled back on the throttles and reduced the power to the one good engine. They lost altitude instantly and rapidly approached the same height as the tropical canopy on either side of the enormous lake.

Decker extended the flaps but there was no need for the landing gear on a water landing. "Let's hope those bastards don't have anything else in store for us."

They all heard the sound of crackling in the distance.

"They're firing again!" Riley called out.

Selena gasped. "You just had to say it, didn't you

Mitch?"

"Huh?"

"If you hadn't said what you just did, we'd be all right."

"That's insane!"

Suddenly the Avalon lurched heavily to the left and began to nosedive.

Selena screamed. "What's happening?"

"Rudder's off! They must have hit the tail!" Decker called out, gripping the yoke as it shook and wobbled violently in his hand. "We have serious issues with some of our control surfaces."

"And this means?"

Decker stared up at her. "See that lake?"

"Yes, of course, I bloody do! It's right in front of us!"

"We might not be landing on it anymore."

The plane twisted in the sky and she gasped again. "What does that mean?"

"It means the damage to the aircraft is moving us off course and I'm struggling to steer her back toward the lake!"

"But the rest is just… jungle!"

"I had *not* noticed that – thanks! Brace for impact, we're going down!"

16

"Can't you take her back up?"

"Ha! You just called the Avalon her!"

"I did not. I merely asked if you could take *it* back up into the air again."

"No can do," he said. "Only one engine and thanks to the damage to the control surfaces, I'll struggle just to keep her on a straight course, never mind up."

"Well fuck me with a bag over my head," Riley said. "This really is bad."

"Yeah," Decker said. "This really is bad. Lena, get back and tell the others to strap in and brace for impact. Riley, you're up front with me. I could use some help with the yoke and rudders. Strap yourself in and enjoy."

"Got it, Mitch."

When Selena had disappeared through the cockpit door, Decker turned to the young Australian. "We're in deep shit, Riley. I didn't want to say anything with Lena around, but if this thing hits the trees we're breaking into a thousand pieces. We might not all walk away."

"Fuck."

"And even if we do, we know we have hostile forces armed with guns in the area, almost certainly Tarántula and his goons. If we're wounded in the crash it's not going to be hard for them to find the site and hunt us down with their weapons."

"Double fuck."

"Grab the yoke and help me pull it across to the left. We're going to do all we can to counterbalance the yaw with full left rudder, got it?"

"Got it."

The tall Australian followed Decker's orders and extended his long leg down until his boot was on the rudder pedal. The effect was instant but did little to correct their trajectory. "You think we're going to make it?"

The engine on their left-hand side growled and roared and the hot tropical wind buffeted the plane back and forth as they plummeted ever-closer to the ground.

"We're not hitting the middle of the lake in a million years, which is what I was going for. We might just be able to make the area to the right near the shore. Our goal right now is to miss those trees."

"I'm with you, mate."

Decker reduced power again and struggled hard against the powerful yaw pulling the aircraft away from the lake and toward the jungle. They were already below the canopy level of the surrounding rainforest and impact was imminent. Decker called out to the crew and told them to brace and seconds later the vintage aircraft touched down on the edge of the lake with a stomach-turning smash. Diana screamed for her life as the plane twisted to the right and plowed a deep groove in the water.

Decker fought it. Full corrective rudder and pulling the remaining engine's power back to idle, he gripped the yoke with his full force and just managed to keep the Avalon heading on a straight course. After a few terrifying seconds, the old plane came to a rest at the end of the lake just inches from the shore in a cloud of smoke and carbon monoxide. Decker and Riley shut the plane down and walked out of the cockpit.

In the main cabin, Diana gasped and grabbed onto Riley's arm as the aircraft bobbed about on the surface of the lake. As the one working prop slowed down above them and the roar of the engine settled down into a much quieter whine, Charlie looked through the window and took in the jungle surrounding the lake. "So when they said this place was remote, they actually meant unbelievably bloody remote."

"Yes," Decker said. "Yes, I think they *did* mean that."

They climbed out of the Avalon and waded through the shallow water around the aircraft, passing their packs of gear from one to the next until it was on the shore. They stacked the heavy backpacks, full of camping equipment, ropes, glow sticks, food, and water, into a big heap and watched the old seaplane bobbing up and down, smoke from its damaged engine rising above them in the moonlight. It drifted above the lake for a few seconds and then the breeze picked it up and it was gone over the tropical canopy. They listened as the sound of the engine quietly faded, to be replaced with the relentless chirping of cicadas and croaking of marsh frogs.

"Well..." Riley said, reaching down for his pack. "Welcome to the —."

"No," Selena said. "Do. Not. Say. It."

He laughed and hoisted the pack up over his shoulders. "You know me too well, Professor Moore."

Decker was surprised to see a smile on Selena's face which she had tried to hide by turning away and pulling her pack out of the pile. No matter what she said, he knew there would always be a special place in her heart for Riley Carr.

Decker waded back into the lake and started examining the aircraft's control surfaces. After a short search, he laughed bitterly in the night. "Son of a bitch! I was right – someone definitely shot us. These are gunshots. Unmistakable."

"But how can that be?" Diana said. "No one can possibly know we're here."

"Local tribes?" Riley asked.

Acosta shrugged. "Perhaps, but highly improbable. The local tribes in this area are certainly some of the most remote in all of Middle America, but they are not known to be hostile."

Decker was wading back to the shore. "Well, someone sure as shit is hostile. My goddam plane is trashed. That's going to take hours to repair, and that's presuming I have the necessary parts in the back of the plane."

"Damn it," Selena said. "This is really going to slow us down."

Atticus said, "If you ask me, it was Tarántula and his men. They took the seal, and someone has clearly translated it for them. They got here before us because they left Xunantunich before us. The rest is history."

"Agreed," Decker said. "And that means they're already here and ahead of us."

"How the hell did they get out here?" Riley asked.

"There are some locations where a chopper can land," Acosta said. "Not many because of the density of the forest. There have been calls to make new clearings but there are many regulations about deforestation here. This is a very special ecosystem and each clearing takes a long time to justify. So, I guess they flew out on a chopper and landed in a clearing somewhere."

"So, how far away is Flower Mountain?" Diana asked.

"Can I see the picture of the seal you took, Charlie?" Selena said.

He handed it over and she frowned. Then, Atticus and Acosta gathered around her and all three of them studied the picture in the beam of a flashlight. "Unfortunately, quite far away," Acosta said at last. "We need to head in this direction."

A gunshot ripped through the night.

"Everyone take cover!" Decker said. "Looks like whoever shot the plane out of the sky isn't done with us yet!"

17

The sound of gunshots cracked in the night, sending countless scarlet macaws flapping out of the canopy above their heads. Decker and Riley had already drawn their weapons and were firing back, but blindly. There was no way to tell where the shooting's point of origin was.

Charlie drew his gun and pulled up beside the Australian. "You know where they are yet?"

"Not a clue, mate."

Decker cleared some foliage away from his face and searched the dark jungle. "And now they seem to have stopped shooting."

Riley nodded. "They don't want to give their position away."

"So what now?" Selena said. "We can't just wait here all night waiting to get shot at. They might be surrounding us or something."

Diana stared into the trees. "I don't like this at all."

"We can't wait here," Riley said. "We might not know their position, but they know ours. We should get the packs and get started into the jungle. Keep quiet and put some distance between us and this place as fast as poss."

"Sounds good to me," Decker said. "Let's get the rest of the packs."

The journey south through the Lacandon Jungle punished the crew members hard. Pathways through the jungle were hard to find and the last three miles of track were pitted with ruts and grooves and other scars of the unforgiving tropical climate. Hours passed and dawn broke quickly, shattering the black night with soft rays of golden sunlight.

They marched on. Most of the way, the jungle closed in over the track, but now they broke through into an exposed section. The temperature difference was stark. Gone was the humid, cloying grip of the jungle, replaced instead by the merciless torture of a white-hot sun, already high in the sky. It pitched down on them with an intensity that felt personal, and Selena began struggling with it straightaway.

"This is as hot as hell."

"Why do you think they call the place Tabasco?" Charlie said.

She faced him and rolled her eyes, making sure he felt her disdain. "Tabasco is miles away, Valentine."

"Oh, is it?"

"Yes. Believe me, yes."

Acosta's boots crunched on the track. "Everywhere is miles away."

"We're nearly there, Lena," Riley said. "Hang in there."

"It's easy for you to say. You probably grew up with worse, right?"

He laughed and smiled at her. His eyes were shaded by a battered wide-brimmed hat he'd picked up in Mexico City. "You could say that." He gave a low whistle and looked out across the canopy of the forest to their right. In front of him, Acosta was carefully navigating an incline in the track and their new elevation allowed a great view across to a hazy western horizon.

Riley watched him go as he replied to Selena's question. "When I was a kid out on the station, it was so hot it could lift up a dead man's dick."

Charlie laughed, but Selena slapped his leg. "Stop being so disgusting."

The Australian SAS corporal gave an innocent shrug. "Hey, welcome to Riley."

"Tell me about it," Selena said. "Haven't heard that one before though."

Acosta had apparently missed the joke, staring hard at the seal and wandering down another incline leading back into the darkness of yet more jungle. The breathtaking view was gone again, and now they were surrounded by endless layers of some of the most ancient and ruthless jungle anywhere on the planet. Exhausted after hours of hiking, the team stopped to remove their packs and drink some water.

"This place really is remote," Diana said.

"Still, look on the bright side," Riley said, pulling his pack up his shoulder and raising his voice. "We could be wherever *you* came from, Mitch."

Selena laughed. "He's already asleep, you berk."

"Asleep?" Charlie said, amazed.

"Yes, and in this jungle, too," Selena said. "How does he do it?"

Riley was shocked, too. "If there's one thing I've learned about Mitch Decker, it's that he could sleep even if he was on a rollercoaster with his arse on fire."

Charlie chuckled. "I'm loving the imagery."

Leaning up against a tree trunk, Decker's face was obscured totally by his Akubra hat, but now he grunted, refolded his arms over his chest, and twisted to get more comfortable.

Acosta got up, rearranged his pack and started walking, gingerly avoiding a pothole caused by the tropical downpours. "We must go. We have no idea where these men are. They could be on our tail, or they might already have found Flower Mountain."

Selena woke a grumbling Decker and they got to their feet and started walking back up the foothills of a mountain range. By the time they caught up with Acosta, he had left the track and wandered down to another lake, this one much smaller than Miramar. When he reached the shore, the Mexican professor started scanning the far side of the lake with a pair of Riley's heavy-duty ex-army field glasses.

Leaving Atticus, Charlie, Diana, and a yawning Decker behind them, Selena and Riley walked over to him down on the lake's northern shore. The shocking density of the jungle had made the latest leg of their journey go on much longer than any of them had expected, and now it was well after noon. At its zenith now, the sun's relentless beating sapped their energy as they made the short walk over to Pepe Acosta.

Reaching a short stretch of pure white sand, Selena pulled up beside him, removed her hat, and wiped the sweat from her forehead. Replacing the hat, she blew out a long, weary breath. "So, we got this far, at least."

The academic nodded but didn't turn to face her. Instead, his eyes remained glued to the binoculars as he spoke. "Si, but is it far enough?"

She stared out across the enormous freshwater lake and tried to take it all in. Surrounded on all sides by the same dense tropical rainforest they had spent the morning hiking through, an enormous mountain rose up on its southern shore. It was a spectacular sight that impressed even Riley.

"That's one fuckin' beautiful lake," he said. "Talk about untouched. I bet it's looked like this since the dawn of time itself."

"Then you'd lose your money," Selena said.

"How so?"

"We know from both quality primary and secondary sources that during the Mayan era this wasn't a lake but a simple lowland valley."

Riley regarded the lake's smooth surface. "You're shitting me?"

"I am not *shitting* you, no," she sighed. "There was once a fabulous city built here, where all this water is right now. A city was built at the base of Flower Mountain. As we said earlier, up until now I believed these stories to be mere legends, but now it looks like they were real."

"Get outta town."

"Historical fact, Carr," she said. "Apparently."

"Well, do me sideways and call me Mother Theresa. I never knew that."

"For *God's* sake, will you stop talking like that!"

"Sorry. I learned to talk in the army. Late developer."

"You can say that again. Anyway, look over there." She raised an arm and pointed off to the right. When she had the attention of both men, she said, "If you look really closely, you can see something protruding just above the surface of the lake."

Acosta swiveled the binoculars over to the location and whistled. "Los cojones! I see something! It looks like stone ruins, but they are barely visible above the surface."

"Precisely," she said. "You are looking at the ruins of the aforementioned ancient Maya city."

Riley shoved his hand under Acosta's face and made a quick beckoning gesture with his fingers. "Let's have the bins, mate."

The Mexican handed them over and wandered off toward a rise leading up into the foothills beyond the lake. Seconds later Riley was scanning the lake for himself. "That, my friends, is absolutely bloody amazing."

"It's why I love archaeology," Selena said. "Who knows what we would find, if we could dive down and search?"

Riley leaned in close and lowered his voice. "Not Pepe's personality, that's for sure."

"Stop it!"

"That baby's MIA."

Over their heads, a brightly colored parrot squawked and screeched and flapped its way out of a tree. Another followed, then dozens more flew up into the bright blue sky. The water lapped at the shore, breaking on the mangroves to their west, and they all heard the familiar cry of a troop of howler monkeys coming from deep inside the rainforest behind them.

"This place could be paradise," Selena said.

"A paradise with crocodiles." Riley handed the binoculars to her. "And that ain't much of a paradise if you ask me."

"Gosh," she gasped. The crocodile was swimming halfway between the shore where they were gathered and the ruins out in the lake. "You don't get those on Bond Street."

"No, you get a different kind of predator there," he said. "Still, he looks hungry."

She laughed. "How the hell can you tell that?"

"Just something about his eyes."

"I found something!" Acosta called out. "A small cave in the side of the Flower Mountain foothill. It must be Xibalba!"

"Cool," Riley said. "We found hell. Excellent. Wait till I tell my mum – she'll be stoked."

"It's not hell," Selena said. "Do try and grow up."

The rest of the crew walked over to them, weary but eyes full of anticipation. Charlie wiped the sweat beading on his forehead with his arm. "Sure feels like hell."

They turned their backs on the lake and walked over to Acosta. The Mexican academic had already disappeared inside the cave. By the time they reached the entrance, he stepped back out with a frown on his face.

"I'm sorry, but it looks like someone else has already

beaten us to it…"

Decker took a step forward and saw a hole inside the cave. He reached for his flashlight but when he got to the edge of the abyss, he noticed a glowstick already nestling down in the dirt. Its soft green glow lit the bottom of the shaft and revealed another slightly larger cave.

"Must be the guys who shot us down," he said, pushing his hat up a little. "Damn."

18

The Snake King fought hard to control his temper. They had been down inside the cave system for an hour already and still, they had not found the Stormbringer. Worse, he knew they had company in the jungle. Last night, they had shot down the Avalon and tried to crash it, but its crew had survived an emergency landing on the lake. They had shot back at his men, so he knew they were alive and kicking. Now, they could be anywhere. If they met again, they would have to be killed.

He heard one of Tarántula's men calling up from a dark abyss and turned to see the younger Mercado brother leaning on the handle of a pickaxe. He looked irritated and tired.

"What did he just say?" the Snake King said.

Tarántula looked at Carlos then back to Miguel. "Qué?"

"It's another slab!"

"Another of the slabs?" Tarántula said.

Novarro and Diablo also stopped their work and faced the boss. They were standing on a large slab of carved rock blocking further access into the cave system.

"Yes, it's another stone slab," Miguel called up. "But big, much bigger than the other one we found earlier."

"How big?" the Snake King said, his frustration rising.

"Hard to say, but judging from the thickness, I'd say maybe fifty square feet."

"Which means we're not getting through it with these." Novarro gave his pickaxe a contemptuous kick with his boot. "Not in a million years."

Diablo spat a wad of chewing tobacco on the edge of the slab and sniffed. "This is wasting our time."

"Then break out the explosives," the Snake King said. "I want this slab out of the way now and no delays! This is the only entrance into Xibalba that we know of. Clearly, someone a very long time ago decided to stop anyone getting down inside this cave system. This tells me we're in the right place. The Stormbringer is here, I can sense it. Now, blow it open!"

"Boss."

Miguel scrambled up out of the hole, walked over to their gear, and pulled out a bag packed with C4 explosives. Glancing at his older brother, he closed the pack and marched back over to the gorge with the bag slung over his shoulder.

As he climbed down and positioned the C4, the Snake King almost felt dizzy. So, the old friar had been right all along! His memoirs weren't just the deranged ramblings of an old fool whose mind had been warped by too much tropical heat. It was all true! Right here, right now, he was about to discover what he had spent half his life searching for.

The terrifying powers of the ancient Maya god, Huracan. All those years of searching had been worth it. All his blood, toil, and sweat were about to reap terrible and unimaginable dividends.

Miguel wiped some sweat away from his forehead. "We're nearly there, boss!"

The Snake King and Tarántula gave each other an anxious look as the men finished carefully placing the plastic explosives in strategic locations around the more exposed sections of the stone slab.

Watching the work come to a finish, the Snake King shook his head in astonishment. "Good God! They buried it under hundreds of thousands of kilos of sandstone. Think of how much it must have terrified them! More than the wrath of God himself!"

Carlos and Miguel caught each other's eye. The two close brothers already knew what the other was thinking. They didn't have to say anything. Tarántula saw the look on his men's faces but turned away. Now was not the time to get nervous.

The last to finish deploying the explosives was Diablo. He had used his pickaxe to widen a channel at the northern edge of the slab and was stuffing the C4 deep inside it. When he finished, he laid down his pickaxe once again and slowly climbed up out of the hole. "All done."

"Then take cover and detonate the explosives!" the Snake King ordered.

The enormous explosion achieved the result they needed, blowing the second slab into smithereens all over the cave floor. When the dust settled, it revealed a gaping hole in the sandstone and beneath it, another long passageway receding into the darkness below. A dozen large black bats flapped and fluttered out of the darkness and buzzed around them for a few seconds before flying away up the entrance tunnel.

"What the hell?" Tarántula said.

Novarro made the sign of the cross. "Camazotz!"

The Snake King's face hardened. "Death bats. I expected them. We are venturing now into their world, the Underworld." The men mumbled and grew restless. Before any of them could speak, the Snake King shouted, "Move on!"

They walked down the passageway for a few moments until reaching a large cavern, inside which were more treasures than any of them had ever seen before. Gold and silver, emeralds and diamonds, golden trays, necklaces, earrings. It went on forever. Tarántula was mesmerized by the hoard and couldn't stop his mind from running wild with the thought of the power so much wealth could buy. He turned to speak to the Snake King but he was already gone.

Scanning the cavern, he found him in the far corner, standing in silence on his own beneath a large colony of black bats hanging off the rocky ceiling. He was in front of an alcove carved into the cave wall, mumbling to himself and trembling with fear. When Tarántula saw what had mesmerized his boss, he felt his heart skip a beat.

Resting on a raised stone slab, he saw a large metallic capstone. It looked like nothing he had ever seen before. Silver, but not silver. Copper, but not copper. Metal yes, but since when did the surface of metal swirl and move around like it was made of water? At its apex was some sort of cap, carved into the shape of Huracan's angry face.

The Snake King was staring into the capstone with blank eyes. The reflection looking back at him was terrifying. His eyes were clear enough, but the rest of his face was obscured by his mask of green jade. Intricately carved snakes fashioned from onyx and turquoise squirmed from the holes carved for his eyes and mouth and gave him a powerful sense of his own royal power. He had discovered the mask himself after an excavation in Calakmul. To the Maya, and him, jade was more precious than gold and until this moment he had coveted the mask more than anything.

He studied the capstone more closely. Movement. Was something moving inside the metal?

He heard himself gasp at the very idea.

Could it be the legends were right all along? Was this polished metal capstone, once the property of the original snake kings, really a portal to another dimension? Could he access the real Underworld with its magic? Would it reveal the future as the legends said? Did it hold demons within its enigmatic heart? And what if the demons inside could climb out into this world? The questions buzzed in his head like static electricity.

He turned away from the capstone. Already, too scared to look again in case he saw something he didn't want to. But then, was this not the whole purpose of his life's mission? He looked back into the polished metal. More of the strange smoke patterns swirled within its shining coppery surface. Smooth and wispy and curling in delicate tendrils and then dissipating into nothing.

His breathing quickened.

"What do you see, boss?"

He heard a voice out of nowhere. He was dimly aware of someone moving beside him.

Tarántula.

"What do you see?"

"This is the capstone we have been searching for," the Snake King said, humbly. "This is the Stormbringer that Montesino described. We have found it. It is mine at last. I have the power."

"Power, sir?"

"Huracan's power. This is my destiny, my loyal servant. Somewhere in this capstone is a power far greater than anything any mortal man could ever imagine."

He stared at the capstone like it was a living, breathing creature, reaching out and stroking it with his fingers. "It's not made of any metal we currently understand, my loyal servant. It's something entirely different. Something completely rare and undiscovered. The ancients gave it a name in their own language which translates roughly as the metal of the gods. I will call it, divinium."

Still stroking the ancient reflective capstone, he marveled at its brilliance in the low light of the flashlights bouncing around in the chamber. It seemed not only to reflect the beams of these flashlights but to soak them up and then radiate them out again several magnitudes stronger. The glowing grew stronger until it was as bright as the midday sun.

"It's beautiful."

He leaned closer and studied himself once more in the strange new metal. His jade mask seemed even brighter and more dazzling inside the capstone. He reached out toward his reflection. Or was his reflection reaching out toward him? He wanted to climb inside and join this other strange world. Walk among the souls in the Underworld. Dance among the demons. Lead them back into this plane and raise the bloodiest hell anyone had ever seen.

Later.

For now, the capstone's ancient power had a more prosaic task.

He leaned closer and his staring intensified until he finally saw it. And heard it. Gunshots. He was knocked from his reverie by the sound of more shooting. He turned and he saw the foreign team of archaeologists. They were charging into the chamber with guns raised, firing on them. Muzzles flashed. Men yelled. Lead flew all over the place. He screamed and threw himself over the capstone.

"No! You mustn't hit it! You'll shatter it! It's too fragile!"

The shooting intensified. He felt a bullet rip into his leg and screamed in pain.

"Boss?"

Breathing as hard as if he had been sprinting, and sweat beading on his forehead, he turned and saw Tarántula. The experienced gangster was staring back at him, terrified. The Snake King screamed again and pointed at the archway. "Get down! They're shooting!"

Tarántula looked confused. "Sir, who is shooting?"

"The other team! Decker. The Moores! They're in

here, they're trying to take the capstone! They're....
they're...."

"There is no one in this cavern but us, sir," said Tarántula. "Carlos, Miguel. Diego and Diablo and some of the other men. Me. No one else."

The Snake King felt his heart pounding in his chest and worked hard to slow his breathing. He felt confused. Dazed. Then, another gasp fled his lips like a frail baby bird when he realized what he was witnessing. Decker and the Moores hadn't charged into the chamber with guns blazing.

Not yet.

"Praise the gods!" he said.

"Sir?"

"Praise the gods, for they have given me the wonderful gift of augury!"

Tarántula frowned. "I don't understand. I thought the capstone gave us the power of Huracan? The power to destroy cities?"

"Indeed it does, my loyal servant, but it has also given another gift. The demons inside this capstone have shown me the future, Tarántula! Our enemies are close and will soon attack us through that archway over there. I saw it all with my own eyes."

Tarántula noticed the way the Mercado brothers were looking at each other. He felt they might be thinking the same thing he was. Had they placed their futures in the hands of a total madman?

"You saw the future, sir?"

The Snake King grew silent. The implications of what he had seen were only just beginning to register in his whirring mind. Drunk with the potential of his new power, he turned and barked at the Mercado brothers.

"Cover it with the tarp," he snapped. "It's important no one looks directly into the capstone!"

"Yes, boss."

"Then prepare the men to get it out of here and back to the chopper. We have a world to destroy."

19

Riley had the most caving experience, and now he set his faithful alloy descender to seventy feet, checked the rig was safe, and switched his flashlight on and off. Good – all was still functioning properly. Peering over the edge of the giant abyss inside the cave, he slid on a pair of rope rescue gloves, gave the rope one final tug to make sure it was secure, and then walked backwards over the edge.

"Take care, Riley!" Diana called out.

"No worries. This is a piece of cake compared with some of the stuff those bastards in the regiment made us do."

Then he gave her a cheeky wink and loosened the rope weaving through the rappel rack to reduce the friction and let it slide through. Then he was gone, plummeting away from them and into the darkness below.

Within seconds, he felt the ambient temperature change around him. He expected this and continued sailing down the side of the rock-hole, using the glowstick down in the dirt below to guide his speed and know when to slow down and land. As the glowstick raced up to meet him, he tightened the rope feeding through the rack and reduced his speed. Then, a few feet from the cave floor, he stopped completely, uncoupled himself from the rigging, and hopped down onto the solid ground.

Flashlight on, he scanned his new surroundings. He was the original class clown when workload permitted, but no one was more serious when the rubber hit the road. Trained to a brutally competent degree by the SASR out in the deserts of Western Australia, he knew what was expected of him when he clocked on to a serious job. This was one of those times.

"You see anything?"

Selena's voice. He stared up at them far above his head. He didn't know why, but looking at the top of a tunnel from the bottom always looked further away than looking at the bottom of a tunnel from the top. A breeze blew on his face and rippled his hair. A slight sulfur smell. Odd.

"Not really," he called back, returning to his examination of the cave. "Regular looking cave with one exit. Looks scary. Someone going to come and hold my hand?"

"I will!" Selena said. "I can't wait to get down there."

"Just hold on a damned second," said Decker. "I'm going down next."

"Why you?"

"I'm an ex-US Marine."

He needed no more words, and moments later he was rappelling down the same line Riley had used. When he hit the ground, he unhitched himself from the rigging and pulled a flashlight with one hand and a pistol with the other.

"G'day, Cap!" Riley said.

"Howdy. We're going to make sure that tunnel is safe before bringing the whole team down here."

"Lena's seen worse – and Charlie too!"

"Sure, but if there's anything ugly in there, we don't need Diana, Atticus, and old man Acosta down here. We're not discussing it."

"No need, Mitch. We're singing from the same hymn sheet when it comes to the old crumblies up there."

"Huh?"

"Atticus and old Pepe."

Decker rolled his eyes. "Crumblies?"

"Just a figure of speech."

The two men walked down the tunnel at the base of the shaft. Gravelly dust crunched under their boots as they inched forward, flashlight beams searching the darkness ahead of them for threats. Ahead, they now saw a cave mouth opening out onto a large cavern. When they reached it, neither of them could believe what they were seeing.

Riley laughed. "You want to tell the others or should I?"

"I'll go."

When Decker returned with the rest of the crew, Riley was already well inside the cavern taking a good look around. He had kicked a path through rocky debris on the cave floor which the others now used to catch up with him. They too were shocked.

Charlie gazed at the chamber, amazed by what he was seeing. "Could there *be* any more gold in this place? There must be hundreds of millions of dollars' worth in here!"

"Maybe it was like some kind of ancient Fort Knox," Decker said.

"No, it's a tribute," said Atticus, sweeping his flashlight over the treasure and up onto the fierce face of a statue in front of them. "Tribute to *him*."

"Who's that guy?" asked Riley.

"Huracan," Selena said, stepping closer and bringing her own flashlight up to the face.

Acosta ran his hands over the base of the towering statue. "Yes! Huracan, the God of Storms. We meet at last... here in Xibalba."

Selena was mesmerized. "This is incredible. This must be where the ancient tribes really thought their Underworld was. In pre-Christian culture, death usually meant the soul going to an afterlife or perhaps being reincarnated, but this changed after the Spanish invasion. The introduction of Christian concepts of the afterlife into Maya culture meant that local tribes began seeing Xibalba as a place of punishment, sort of analogous to our concept of hell. That was *here*!"

"So we really are in hell?" Charlie said.

Diana shivered. "I don't like this place at all. It gives me the creeps."

"Not me," Riley said. "I love all this Aztec stuff!"

"How many more times do I have to tell you, Riley?" Selena sighed. "This is Maya!"

He scratched his head. "Oh, yeah. Keep forgetting. What's the difference again?"

"There are many differences. For one, the Aztecs were chiefly concerned with offering the human heart to the gods." Selena continued to mull around the cavern, lighting objects of interest with her flashlight as she spoke. "They thought this was the ultimate symbol of sacrifice, but the Maya were different. For them, the supreme offering to the gods was human blood. Another critical difference was that Maya used to inflict horrendous torture on their victims before death and often skinned them after the sacrifice so the priest, or *chilan*, could wear their skin while the worshippers danced."

"And the victims were alive while the hearts were ripped out, right?" Riley asked.

"Oh, yes," Selena said casually. "The Maya used to slice a hole in their abdomens and pulled the heart out from the bottom of the ribcage, all while the victim was alive, kicking and screaming."

"They sound delightful," Diana said with disgust.

"And it gets worse," Selena said. "Archaeologists once found a grave with various sacrifice victims in it, including some children as young as three. They analyzed the skeletons and found they had been flayed, stabbed, and dismembered."

"I've heard enough," the Portuguese woman said, genuinely upset by what she was hearing.

Riley had also gone quiet. "Yeah, I reckon that's enough history for one day."

"So, where's this notorious doomsday machine?" Charlie said, his voice loud in the quiet cavern. "I mean, that's why we're here, right?"

"Right," Selena said. "So keep looking."

"Hey!" Acosta called out from the far side. "Come over here! I think I found something."

20

"What is it, old man?" Atticus said.

"Look inside this alcove." Acosta lit it with his flashlight. "It's another series of glyphs featuring what I'm presuming is the Stormbringer."

Atticus looked closer and saw what looked like a carving of an ancient Maya capstone surrounded by strange golden rays as if it were the rising sun. "A capstone?" he said, twisting his head back around to his friend in astonishment. "Could it be the Stormbringer was some sort of capstone?"

"I think it might be!" Acosta said. "And not just any capstone – this image clearly represents the main temple at Xunantunich!"

"The missing capstone at Xunantunich!" said Selena. "Of course!"

Amidst the high fives and excitement, Charlie frowned. "Wait. Just what were these capstones used for anyway?"

Selena calmed down and said, "Most of the bigger Maya buildings, especially those used as temples and palaces, were always very complex and intricately designed. They often had parts of the structure with corbelled roofing, and…"

"What sort of roofing?" Charlie asked. "Soldier here, not an architect."

"Sorry. Corbelled roofing means built-in arches."

"Take the classic corbel vault," Atticus said. "This is an integral part of Maya architecture which they used all the time to support roofs and upper stories. We see an example of it here inside this alcove. It's a more basic technique than properly curved arches, but it worked wonders for the Maya."

"Got it."

"Anyway," Selena continued with a proud smile from her father, "the bigger structures like palaces and temples used the corbelled roofing techniques, which involved overlapping flat stones in such a way they would meet up at the top of the arch. This would then be spanned with a capstone. If you're interested, you can see a wonderful example in the burial chamber of King Pakal."

"I'll take your word for it," Charlie said. "But thanks."

"I had no idea the Maya were such intrepid architects," Diana said.

"Oh yes," Atticus said, rounding on her and removing his glasses to reveal keen eyes sparkling with enthusiasm. "They had it all – vaulted roofs, shady colonnades, multi-story towers, not to mention steam rooms and lavatories. Today we think we created everything. We might give a vague nod to ancient Rome, but everywhere else means nothing."

He stared back inside the alcove and looked once again at the picture of the capstone. "They even had specially carved doorways, often in the shape of a monster's mouth. These represented portals into different realms." The ghost of a smile lingered on his face. "Exciting, no?"

"I guess so," she said. "But maybe not the part about walking through monsters' mouths to reach other worlds."

"They were a very mystical culture," Atticus said, thrusting his free hand in his pocket and giving a long, soft sigh. "Sometimes, I wish I had a time machine. Then I could go back and actually *live* among people like the ancient Maya, or the citizens of Mohenjo-Daro, or ancient Athens! Think what that would be like!"

"A world without hot, running water, flushing toilets or deodorant," Charlie said. "Very mystical."

Atticus's smile faded. "You haven't a romantic bone in your body, have you, Mr. Valentine?"

"Maybe not, but I can field strip an assault rifle in less than sixty seconds and I'm a total devil when it comes to making Thai kaeng khae curry. We all have our uses."

Atticus tipped his head. "And a very valuable member of our team you are, too."

Decker removed his hat to wipe some sweat from his eyes. "Can we get back to the capstone? Remember, those maniacs are probably down here somewhere!"

"Thank you, Mitch," Selena said. "The point is that while Xunantunich is a very well preserved ancient site, it has many missing parts, and it looks like this capstone was once part of the temple roof there. If Montesino really did see what he described in his journal, it's possible the destructive power he witnessed was somehow channeled by the capstone."

"I'll ask the obvious one," Riley said. "How?"

She shrugged. "I'm an archaeologist, not a scientist."

"But what if it's not science?" Diana asked. "What if it's some sort of divine power beyond our imagination?"

Charlie scoffed. "You can't be serious? There's no such thing! If it really was the capstone that caused the devastation Montesino wrote about, then there has to be a perfectly rational, scientific explanation."

"If you say so," Diana said, taking a step back from the alcove.

Decker scratched his jaw. "Fine, and it's all great that we found these pretty pictures of the capstone, but where's the real thing? Answers on a postcard and gratefully accepted."

"Ah, that we still don't know," Atticus said, holding a wobbling flashlight in his old hand as he stared up at the alcove. "But this is something else! Already it's one of the greatest moments of my career and we've barely scratched the surface."

Selena drew up beside him and swept the beam of her own flashlight across the alcove's ornate stone ceiling. "Postclassic era?"

He nodded. "I should say so. Certainly doesn't seem to be any evidence of the post-contact era or Spanish conquest in here."

"What does that mean to us plebs?" Charlie said.

"It means it was built between five hundred and a thousand years ago," Decker said.

Selena and Atticus turned simultaneously and stared at him. "You amaze me," she said.

He shrugged. "I do listen to some of your ramblings… occasionally."

"You flatter me, Mitch. Please stop."

He grinned. "But that's the limit of my knowledge."

Diana said, "It's a very pretty alcove, I agree, but…"

"But it's still not what we're looking for," Selena said. "It's nothing close to what we're looking for. At least now we know the Stormbringer seems to be somehow contained in a capstone as you'd see on the top of a pyramid."

"Wait," Atticus said. "You see that glow over there in the next cavern?"

"I do indeed," said Decker. "And I don't like it. What the hell could be glowing like that in a place like this?"

Atticus shrugged and swallowed nervously. "Not a fire."

"No, not a fire," Riley said. "Not unless it's been burning for half a millennium."

"Which it has not," said Charlie. "Whatever the hell it is."

"Please do not use that word," Diana said with a

shudder. "Remember where we are!"

"C'mon, Di!" Riley said. "Don't you start, too. Just because we're in a cave in Xibalba where the ancients said the entrance to hell was located, doesn't mean this is the actual entrance to hell, right Lena? Right? I mean, does it?"

She thought about her reply. "Not sure on that one, Riley. To be honest, I'm as much in the dark as you are."

"Let's stop being silly," Atticus said. "Yes, the ancient Maya said the entrance to Xibalba was to be found in a cave in this approximate area. But let's use some deductive reasoning. Just because there is a fiery glow emanating from a cave here does not mean it's the entrance to hell!"

"No, it does not," Decker said. "All we have to do is walk in that cave and find out what it is."

Charlie craned his neck forward and looked deeper into the bright golden glow lighting the cave walls. "And I'm sure when Riley gets back he'll give us a full report of what he found in there and then we can proceed safely."

Riley looked at him. "Wait, what?"

The glow suddenly went out and they heard boots crunching on the cave debris. Selena gasped and swung her flashlight up in front of her. She was horrified to see a man in a jade stone mask in the entrance to the next cavern. Beside him, what looked like a number of common thugs and gangsters. Four of them were carrying something heavy and hidden from view by a large tarp. Then, they saw the Avalon crew and pulled up fast, drawing weapons.

"Drop your guns! Now!" one of them shouted.

Decker looked at Selena. Everyone could see they were massively outgunned and stood little chance in a fire fight. Reluctantly, they dropped their weapons and kicked them over to their captors.

"We finally meet," said Decker. "I've been waiting to get a better look at the assholes who shot up my plane!"

"Yes, an unfortunate necessity," said the masked man. He stepped into their flashlights and stared at them through the slits in his mask.

"Who the hell are you?" Atticus said indignantly. "Coming in here and threatening the life of my daughter, of my friends!"

"But life is full of surprises, old friend." The man slowly removed the jade mask. "Wouldn't you agree?"

When Atticus saw the man's face he gasped and took a step back, reaching out for something to steady himself on. "My God! I don't believe it."

21

"Nate!" Atticus took a further step back in horror. "What the hell is going on? I thought you were in Spain? What the hell is all this about?"

Nathaniel Danvers stepped closer to them, still gripping the jade mask in his hand. "Hell is an unwise word to use in this space, Atticus. You of all people should know that."

Atticus looked behind his old rival and saw the men holding the tarp. "Is that the capstone?"

Danvers laughed. "Ha! So the Moores worked out the Stormbringer was a capstone. Whatever next?"

"Why have you done this? Who are these people?"

"They are my loyal servants, and I am here to claim my destiny!"

Atticus furrowed his brow. "What do you mean by that?"

Another laugh. "I mean the capstone's power is mine to wield and mine alone!"

"This guy's crazy," Riley said.

Charlie nodded. "You can say that again. Just check out that mask!"

Atticus was starting to agree. He turned to Danvers. "But how could you? You're a good man! An academic of the highest quality. What do you mean this power is yours to wield and what was that glowing we all saw?"

Tarántula raised his gun and started to explain, but Danvers stopped him in his tracks by pushing him out of the way and taking a step toward Atticus. "It is not your concern what is happening here, old man. I do not need to explain myself to you. It is enough for you to know that I am not merely an archaeologist. I am the direct descendant of the ancient snake kings and I am here to claim my rightful inheritance and that is the end of the matter. No more questions or I will shoot both you and your daughter."

Atticus stepped forward and started to roll up his sleeve. "You threaten my daughter? Why, I ought to…"

Selena reached out and pulled her father back by his elbow. "Enough, Dad! Can't you see he's serious?"

"As am I, Lena! You won't get away with this, Nate! I'll see to it every university in the world hears about this. You'll lose tenure, you do realize that?"

Carlos and Miguel Mercado burst out laughing, as did the other armed men standing behind them. Finally, Danvers grinned as well.

"I don't think I'm going to need tenure anymore, old man," he said. "When we're done with this business I will retire a very rich man. Maybe buy my own island somewhere. If you're lucky and you ask me nicely enough, perhaps I will hire you and let you serve me drinks."

The laughter increased, an insane burst of giggles in the damp cool of the cave system. Carlos took a step toward Selena. He reached out his hand and brushed it across her chest. "Maybe you can come and serve me drinks on that island, too."

She moved to slap him but Decker grabbed her hand and pulled her back in the same way she had done with her father moments earlier. "Leave it, Lena. These guys don't even need an excuse."

Carlos produced a pistol from his holster and pushed the muzzle up into her forehead. "You should listen to your friend, bitch. He knows what he's talking about. I could fill you full of lead right now and there is nothing anyone here could do to stop it." He leaned in closer and whispered in her ear. "Nothing at all."

Miguel laughed. Diablo lit a cigarillo and puffed a cloud of smoke out, eyes crawling all over Diana.

"So what now?" Decker asked, moving in front of the Portuguese woman.

"That's easy." Danvers refitted the jade mask and started laughing. With the mask on, Nathaniel Danvers was gone. Now he was the Snake King. "Now is easy."

The men laughed nervously.

"Now, you will be taken into the boneyard down here and killed."

"My God!" Atticus said. "You're criminally insane! How could I not have noticed before?"

"Boneyard?" Selena asked, confused. "What boneyard?"

"Don't you know?" the Snake King said. "Down here in Xibalba the demons eat humans like it's going out of fashion. When we arrived, we found piles of human bones covered in gnaw marks... the marks of human teeth."

"That's impossible," Selena said. "The Maya culture was never seriously cannibalistic."

"So we thought," he said smugly. "But now there is evidence to suggest that at the very end of the Maya era there was widespread cannibalism among their people. Archaeologists even found human remains that show arms and legs being torn from their sockets with great force and even with human gnaw marks on them."

Atticus frowned. "There is some evidence the Aztecs practiced cannibalism, mostly tied up with their bloodletting rituals, but even that's fairly scarce and weak. There's much less evidence of cannibalism in the Maya culture apart from what we've already discussed."

"It's of no matter," the Snake King said. "You will go there now. It will be your final resting place, and you should consider this a great honor."

"We're not going anywhere!" Charlie said. "Bloody psychos!"

"Yes, you are!" he snapped. "You will not defy the Snake King!"

"Make us," Decker said.

"Then we will make you! All except *you*, Atticus. You will be my insurance policy. Not only will you stop any of your friends here from causing any further trouble with us, but your archaeological knowledge may come in useful, too."

Atticus laughed. "I see! You need me now. Well, you know what you can do, right?"

"Yes, order you to obey or I will kill your daughter. I need you Atticus. There are very few specialists in Mayan hieroglyphics, even today. You are one of them. Just pray when I no longer need you, I decide to let you go and not have you killed, too."

An enraged Decker lunged at the Snake King. He made no more than a few yards before Miguel Mercado piled into him and sent him tumbling over. His face hit the cave floor and skidded to a grazed, bruised stop a few feet along the newly cleared path. Inches above his head, a bullet split the damp air, blew his hat off, and ripped a chunk of stone from the alcove. When he looked up he saw Novarro standing over him with a smoking gun in his hand.

"Please, give me another chance to blow your head off."

"Maybe later." He flipped over onto his back, spat a wad of dust and debris out of his mouth, and leaned up on his elbows.

"Anyone seen my hat?"

"Here."

He looked to his right and saw his battered Akubra

spinning like a frisbee. Selena had thrown it to him.
"Thanks."
"Welcome!"
"Get up!" the Snake King snarled. "Any more tricks like that and I'll…"
"Kill me?" Decker's face broke into a dark smile. "That little threat runs out of currency when you're already marching a man to his death, asshole."
"Not necessarily," the Snake King hissed. "My loyal Tarántula here is an extraordinarily deranged serial killer. He can find ways to make your death last days, weeks even. Eventually, you will beg him to kill you fast. If you prefer, I can order your days to end in a much more brutal way than a simple bullet to the head."
"You're a bastard, Nate," Atticus said firmly. "A total bastard who is going to regret doing this to us very much."
"I am the Snake King, and you are a sniveling nobody. Now, march!"

22

Diana spoke very little as they approached the boneyard. Nothing in her life had ever prepared for something like this and she was at a loss for words. She was an educated woman. She knew what this world was all about. Her knowledge of history was good, including a reasonable understanding of the Maya and Aztec cultures. But this was something else. The sight of the gnawed, broken human bones piled up all over the place dragged her from her comfort zone and made her feel sick to her stomach.

Surrounded by the heaps of bones, Selena looked around the grisly subterranean cemetery and saw an enormous stone altar. Carved in the traditional Maya style, with stone snakes twirling around the faces of various gods, its intricate altarpiece stretched halfway to the cave ceiling. Beneath it was a beautiful *predella*, in front of which was a smooth stone *mensa*. This was the flat table on top of the main altar stone and now the Snake King's men walked the object they were carrying over to it and set it down.

"Are we to be treated to a show?" Atticus said.

The Snake King laughed. "I don't want to miss seeing your daughter and her friends die, Atticus, but if you think I would let this out of my sight for one second, you are insane."

Riley laughed. "And when a man in a jade mask who thinks he's a lizard king says you're crazy, you really are crazy."

Atticus lunged at the Snake King, but Novarro pulled him away. "Bastard!"

"Remove the tarp!" the Snake King ordered. "Let them see the greatness before they die!"

Selena watched Carlos Mercado pad over and pull it off, revealing something resembling a copper pyramid. But that wasn't quite right, was it? She looked closer again and saw its surface shifting and rolling as if there were smoke or water under its metallic surface.

"What the hell is that thing?" Decker asked.

"That's our capstone," she said, her voice almost a whisper.

"But why does it look like it's moving?" Diana asked. "What is that, moving around like oil on top of the metal?"

"It's not on top of it," Selena said, mesmerized. "It seems to be under the surface."

"Impossible," Charlie said. "Unless it's some sort of glass and we're seeing something moving underneath the surface."

"It's not glass," said Decker. "You can see it's metal. That's obvious, even from back here."

Riley frowned. "Then how do you explain the movement?"

The American shrugged. "Don't ask me. I'm just the flyboy."

"Seriously guys," Charlie said. "What the hell is going on with that thing?"

Selena thought about the question for a moment then looked at her father. "Can it be?"

Atticus furrowed his brow. "It could be."

The Snake King followed their conversation with amusement. "Go on..."

"You really think so, Dad?" Selena asked.

"I do. What about you?"

"Maybe, yes."

Decker sighed. "Do either of you two care to tell the

rest of us just what the hell you're talking about?"

"Please, Mitch," Selena said. "No profanity."

He narrowed his eyes. "I know what you're doing."

"What am I doing?"

"You're trying to annoy me. You're doing it on purpose."

She folded her arms over her chest and squared up to him. "And just why would I do such a childish thing as that?"

"Because of what I said earlier about me being the team leader."

"Stop being so ridiculous."

"Then tell me what the *hell* you're talking about!"

Selena and Atticus relented, answering together: "Mirrors!"

Decker said, "Mirrors?"

"Ha!" the Snake King smacked his hands together. "Mirrors!"

"Yes, mirrors," Selena said. "Mirrors played an important part in all Mesoamerican culture, including Maya culture."

"Is that why they had such cool face-painting?"

"Riley?"

"Yeah?"

"Be gone."

"Sorry."

Decker sighed. "You were saying…"

"I was talking about the important role mirrors played in ancient Mesoamerican culture, and it wasn't about make-up or haircuts." She looked at Riley and scowled. "Mirrors were highly sacred objects, believed to be portals into the underworld. The ancient Mayans used them for scrying."

The Snake King began walking around the capstone, admiring it, stroking it. Still amused by the conversation.

Charlie looked confused. "Don't know that one."

"Augury," Acosta said darkly.

"Exactly," said Selena. "It's the custom of looking into certain media in the hope of communicating with the other side. Over the centuries, most cultures have done this and used all sorts of things – obsidian, polished metal, even the surface of the water."

"As in crystal ball gazing?" he said.

"Exactly. The Maya thought that they could communicate with demons through their mirrors and summon them into this world. They even wore mirrors on their backs in battle in case their enemy tried to attack from behind in the hope the demons would crawl out of the mirror and kill their attackers!"

The Snake King stopped walking and turned. In his hand, he now brandished a gleaming pistol. "Yes, you have shown us all how clever you are, but sadly now it is time for you to die!"

"So this is it?" Diana said with a sniff. "We die here in his *hellscape* and no one will ever know?"

"Are you freaking kidding me, mate?" Riley said. "I'm not dying down here. The Eagles are in the Grand Final this year! I'm not missing that because some barking mad apeshit wackadoodle thinks he's descended from the lizard kings!"

"Snake Dynasty," Selena said with a sigh. "They're not actual lizards. We talked about this."

"Yeah, whatever. They all go down the same way when you hit them hard enough."

The Snake King laughed. "Big words from a man seconds from his own death. Now, you all die. Tarántula! Have your men execute them, now!"

Carlos and Miguel Mercado brought up their submachine guns, smiles on their faces and fingers wrapping around the triggers.

"Mitch!" Selena said. "I've heard of cutting it fine, but don't you think this is a little relaxed even for you?"

"Take it easy," Decker said. "We're not going down without a fight."

"So what are we going to do?" Charlie asked. "We're outmanned and they have our guns!"

"Leave it to me," Decker said. "I have a plan."

23

"He has a *plan*," Acosta said. "This makes me feel much better."

"Cool it with the attitude, *Pepe*," Decker said, raising his voice. "You know, you're a real pain in the ass!"

Acosta was shocked. "But…"

The ex-marine squared up to him. "Ever since this mission began it's been one long brag about how goddam great you are!"

"But this is not true! I…"

"And now look at us! You went and got us killed!"

Atticus's jaw fell open. "How dare you, Captain Decker! Dr. Acosta is one of the very finest archaeologists I have ever had the honor to know!"

"Yeah, yeah," Decker said, turning his hand into a flapping mouth. "Dr. Acosta and his Montesino Codex, Dr. Acosta and his Xunantunich glyphs, Dr. Acosta and his stupid, ancient book of goddam Maya priest incantations, Dr. Acosta and his great big flapping mouth and his…"

"Wait!" the Snake King stepped forward and used his hands to push the barrels of the Mercados' guns down to the floor. "Wait! What did you just say, Captain Decker?"

Decker turned from an angry and confused Felipe Acosta and faced the Snake King. "Huh?"

"I asked you what you just said…*to him.*"

Decker feigned ignorance and smiled broadly. "Don't tell me, you've also had the experience of his big, flapping mouth?"

The Snake King's eyes began to bulge. "What did you

say to him about incantations!?"

"Oh, that..." Decker looked disappointed. "I thought you and I could start some sort of club, right? We could have little t-shirts with *I survived Felipe Acosta* written on them and..."

The Snake King grabbed Carlos Mercado's gun and held it to Decker's temple. "Felipe, what is this book of incantations? Please realize this man's life depends on the answer."

Acosta was dumbfounded and worked his mouth without any sound coming out of it.

Luckily, Selena had already worked out what Decker was doing. "It's nothing," she said, playing it down. "Just an old parchment covered in gobbledygook. Not worth your time. Rubbish. Drivel, really. Just some nonsense about summoning gods and storms. Just hokum, nothing to interest a serious mind like yours."

The Snake King's eyes had filled with greed. "Where did you get this parchment?"

"In the convent," Atticus said, now onboard with the gambit. "It was beneath the Montesino Codex. Held flat under it. My daughter's right. It's just mumbo jumbo, Nate."

"I am not Nate! I am the Snake King!" He pushed the submachine gun's muzzle harder against Decker's temple. "The Snake King!"

Atticus took a step back, eyes widening in fear. "Yes, of course. My mistake, *Snake King*."

The Snake King calmed down. "Where is this Codex? Hand it over!"

"It's not *here*, silly," Selena said.

"Why not?"

"Like we just said, it's nonsense. We saw no reason to bring it along. It would only weigh us down."

Weigh us down, Decker thought with an eye roll.

"What she means is, we didn't want to damage it for no reason so we left it someplace safe."

"What place?"

As she spoke, Riley was making his way closer to Novarro, one eye on his gun.

Selena played along. "Actually, it's in a safe."

"I am losing patience," the Snake King said. "I want the location, now!"

Riley fired his elbow into Novarro's face just as Decker smashed the Snake King's gun away from his temple, grabbing hold of it.

Tarántula saw what had happened and raised his gun but Decker was one step ahead. He squeezed the trigger and swept the muzzle across the cavern, spraying bullets everywhere. Tarántula and the Mercados were first to hit the deck. Novarro and Diablo grabbed the Snake King and Atticus and pulled them to the ground behind the capstone. Then, all of them returned fire on Decker and Riley and drove them into cover.

His gambit had failed. The men had scrambled to cover before anyone else on the Avalon crew was able to get hold of a weapon and the Snake King still had Atticus. Now, Diablo put a gun to Atticus's head and the firing stopped.

The Snake King got to his knees and dusted himself down. "Impressive, but at the same time pathetic. Tarántula! Have your men get the capstone out of here at once. Then I want everyone to evacuate and blow the roof. There's a lot of water in the lake above this cave system. More than enough to drown all of you like the rats you are."

Decker watched as the Mercado brothers removed the capstone and then dragged Atticus out of the complex. To give the old guy credit, he kicked and screamed and fought across every inch, but the gangsters were much stronger. They were all gone a few minutes later, leaving only the Snake King and Tarántula.

"The charges, Tarántula!"

The man from Acapulco put the C4 into three strategic locations around the cave and then the two men walked over to the entrance.

"Goodbye, Avalon crew," the Snake King said. Tarántula was already up the rope ladder and now the Snake King turned and began the ascent. As his feet climbed up out of sight, Selena turned to Decker.

"So what now? Do we disarm the C4?"

"As soon as that psycho hits the detonator," Riley said, "that C4 is turning into a giant fireball. Thing is, we don't know when he's going to push the button."

"Riley's right," Decker said. "The best advice is to get as far away from the explosives as we can and take some sort of cover. That way…"

It was too late. All three packs of C4 exploded in a fierce fireball, blasting chunks of rock and smoke into every corner and shaking the entire cave beneath their feet.

24

"Jeez, who farted?"

Riley's voice sounded muffled in the smoke. All around him, debris slowly fell back to earth and for a few seconds, he wondered if they were going to make it. Then he felt water on his forehead.

"Um, you guys all right?"

They all checked back in, coughing and spluttering.

"That's good, but I think we're in trouble."

"Danvers's plan worked?" Selena called back.

"Let's put it this way, raindrops are falling on my head."

"Mine too," Diana said.

"And me," said Decker. "Look at the cave ceiling! Now the smoke is clearing, I can see at least three giant cracks and they're all getting worse. Danvers's plan worked. The entire lake is going to come crashing down on us any second."

"So what do we do?" Acosta said.

"We wait," said Riley, earning him a strange look from the Mexican academic.

"Wait?" Selena said. "They're holding my father hostage and getting away with the capstone, plus we're about to have a lake crash down on top of us! We need to move!"

"No, I agree with Riley," Decker said. "We wait, but somewhere safer than this."

"I don't understand," said Acosta.

"It's simple." Decker began climbing up to a ledge running around the south side of the cavern. "When that roof falls in, it's going to bring millions of tons of rock and water crashing down into this cavern. We get caught in that and we're dead. But, if we can survive the initial collapse we should be able to ride the surface of the water up to a higher level in the cave complex and find another tunnel that leads us to safety."

"You mean, use the water like an elevator?' Acosta said.

"Exactly, and then…"

The time for an explanation was over. The cracks in the ceiling had joined up and now broke open completely. Water rushed down through them and crashed into the floor. It grew heavier and faster and then reached the edges of the cavern. Seconds later, it was as high as their ledge.

"Get into the water!" Decker screamed. "We can swim out of here over there! I see some sort of tunnel opening up just behind where one of the cracks formed!"

They rode the water up to the tunnel and then climbed up over the ledge. With the water rushing up behind them, they sprinted along the passageway. This was narrower than those that had come before it and much lower. Riley was the tallest in the group and was now having to tip his head forward and hunch his shoulders to make his way through it.

"Can't wait for *this* to end," he said with humor. "This place is literally a pain in the neck."

"We must be nearly there by now," Selena said. "Oh…"

Ahead was a large stone bridge stretching across a wide canyon. Flowing underneath it, they saw a thick, wide channel of bubbling, flowing lava.

Charlie pulled up. "I told you… hell!"

Decker skidded to a halt beside him. "I think we're going over that bridge."

Diana was horrified. "You think we should walk over a rickety wooden bridge a hundred meters above a river of lava? Are you totally insane?"

"On second thoughts, you're right," Decker said. "Forget that. Let's flap our wings and fly across instead."

The Portuguese academic rolled her eyes and sighed. "There is no need to be... what is the word... *faceto!*"

"I don't know what that means," Decker said, "But I know there's no other way across this ravine unless we take the bridge."

"I agree," Charlie said. "And I'm sure when Riley gets back, he'll give us a full report of what he found on the other side, and then we can proceed safely."

Riley scratched at his stubble and grinned. "What is it with you mate? You want me to die or something?"

"Absolutely not," Charlie said. "I need you to get back here alive and tell us if the bridge is safe or not."

"Who knew you were so funny," Riley said. "Not me, that's for sure. Or anyone else. Ever."

"Just greasing the wheels," the former soldier said. "I'll go across first."

"No, you won't," Decker said. "I'm going first."

Selena pulled her head back and stared at him, wide-eyed. "And why you?"

Decker pushed his hat up and wiped the sweat from his eyes. "Because I am obviously the team leader, and that's what team leaders too. We don't let our team members do anything we wouldn't be prepared to do first."

"All good," she said. "Except I am clearly the team leader!"

Riley sighed. "Have you two not organized this yet? I thought you settled all this a long time ago?"

"We have," Decker said. "And..."

"I'm the boss," both he and Selena said together.

"In that case, I'm assuming command," Acosta said.

"In the absence of any sanity, Doctor Felipe Acosta to the rescue! Now get out of my way... I'm going in!"

"Pepe, no!" Selena said, taking hold of his elbow. "Please! Let Mitch go first."

But Decker was already on his way, brushing past Acosta and pushing down on the boards with his right boot to test their strength. He spent another minute pulling on the wooden support towers and guide ropes. They were old and frayed but seemed firm enough. When he stood on the first board, the entire structure groaned and creaked and swayed a little from side to side.

Selena gasped. "I don't think this is a good idea, Mitch. The heat from the lava must have severely damaged this bridge over so many years."

"It's hundreds of feet down," he called back, peering over the side at the flowing magma so far below him. "Any damaging effect it might have would be too greatly reduced by the distance, no matter how long it's been here."

"It's still crazy," she said. "We need to find another way over."

"There's no other way!" he yelled, and the others followed him across the old bridge. On the other side, the shaken team took a few seconds to get their breath back and searched for the next part of their escape route.

"Any ideas?" Charlie said.

"Here!" Selena yelled. "Look at this carving in the rock. It's showing us the way out."

Riley stared at it, confused. "Eh? Just looks like a tangled mess to me. What does it all mean?"

Selena said, "As I said before, the Maya believed the universe was divided into three separate realms, heaven, the earth, and the underworld. Each of these different kingdoms was connected by a giant tree with its roots down in the underworld and the trunk in the earth and then the canopy and leaves up in the heavens. It's best to think of these realms as three separate, existential planes. This part here is clearly the trunk and it's showing us to go this way."

Riley scratched his head. "I'll leave the thinking part to you, Lena."

They followed the path until they saw light. Moments later, they marched out of the underground cave system and into the diffused lighting of the forest floor. All around them insects and birds chirped and cried out in the sweat-streaked humidity. It was another world. Through the canopy, a stormy sky bubbled with dark gray clouds.

"We made it!" Charlie said. "I don't believe it."

"We didn't all make it," Decker said. "We lost a man. We need to get Atticus back. Let's get moving!"

"I agree, but…" Diana collapsed down on one of the boulders on either side of the entrance and sighed deeply. "The heat is too much for me. In Porto, we have drier heat. This is like trying to walk through a bowl of *caldo verde*."

"Eh?" Riley said.

"Hot soup."

"Ah – gotcha!"

"I blame Camaxtli," Acosta said.

"Eh?' said Charlie.

"The Maya god of fate Camaxtli, who brought fire to our world…"

"No more Maya gods," Diana said. "Please."

"All right," Decker said. "We wait here for a few minutes to let everyone get their breath back and then we get back to the lake."

"And pray Danvers hasn't trashed the plane, right mate?" said Riley.

Decker looked at him, horrified. "I never thought of that!"

"C'mon," Selena said. "We really must get going.

Think of Dad."
And then they were on their way.

*

Riley Carr knew all about the jungle. Making corporal in the Australian SAS was no cakewalk. Selection to get into the training program lasted three weeks. 130 men sign up for selection and 104 of them go home bruised and disappointed. After this section of the course follows another 18 months of courses that must be passed before they join a squadron with the rank of junior trooper.

This is called the reinforcement cycle. Here, Riley got the hard stuff. Heavy and light weapons training, parachuting, combat survival, demolitions work, urban combat, patrolling techniques, medic training, signals training, ingress training. Then he was posted to a saber squadron where he specialized. Some specialized as medics, others as signallers or even linguists. Riley chose to be an explosives expert.

Here in his saber squadron, he started a three-year cycle of further training and operations. This was a time of developing the skills already taught, advanced conventional warfare training, and clandestine ops. Explosive ingress techniques, confined-space assaults, building clearance, and close-quarter battle techniques.

With all these years of reinforcement training under his belt, Riley Carr, the young man from an isolated outback station, was finally badged as a full member of the Australian SASR. He finally won the world-famous tan beret and winged dagger insignia badge and joined the regiment, one of only ten percent of the original cohort to do so.

After these years of training, Riley was confident there wasn't a building, ship, plane, train, or oil rig he couldn't break into and clear. And he was more than comfortable engaging the enemy in any terrain. Snow, desert, scrub, savannah, maritime, urban.

Or jungle.

He had spent many a hot, sweaty week on exercise in the dense, steamy jungles of Papua New Guinea, just off Australia's north coast. The PNG Government had a long-standing arrangement with Canberra to allow the Australian Defence Force to train on their territory and Riley had been up there on many occasions, sometimes pitted against other Special Forces guys. All good fun, mate. No problem.

But today he had problems.

While he could spend all day playing with the Snake King and his men if he was on his own, only Mitch Decker had any serious jungle time under his belt. Charlie was a soldier, but he was a former military policeman with mostly urban experience. As for Selena, Atticus, and Diana, or Acosta... they would stand zero chance in a place like this if they got lost or injured, and both were a serious possibility if a firefight broke out.

He marched on, chatting with his friends but always keeping an eye out for trouble. Hours later, they reached their destination and he gave a silent prayer of thanks. Up ahead, Decker made the lake shore first and took cover behind a giant fan palm as he scanned the area for any sign of Danvers and his men. The Avalon was still bobbing about on the surface, badly damaged from the initial attack but from the look of things, not suffering any further problems.

"All right," the American said, breaking cover. "We've got a lot of work to do if we're going to get the Avalon into the air again. I'll get my tools from the cargo hold. Then we get airborne, rescue Atticus and secure the capstone."

Selena put her hands on her hips and blew some hair out of her eyes. "But where the hell do we start? We don't have a clue where they've gone!"

Charlie grinned and shook his phone. "*We* might not, but I know a man who might."

25

Havana, Cuba

The short flight over the dark blue waters of the Caribbean Sea was mostly smooth and enjoyable, even in a vintage plane designed and built long before many of the comforts brought by modern aviation. They flew through the hottest part of the day and crossed into Cuban airspace just as the sun was starting to sink behind them. As the hypnotic hum of the old radial engines lulled the others to sleep, Selena stared through her window and watched the sunset light endless sugarcane fields a deep, welcoming amber.

She gave a quiet sigh and felt the aircraft begin its descent. The agricultural landscape of the island's western provinces slowly melted into farms then villages then conurbations. Lines of tobacco bushes on the rich red soil of Pinar del Rio were smoothly replaced by jumbles of buildings connected by quiet country roads. Further to the south, a heat shimmer rippled over the Mayabeque hills, already distorted by the blue haze of twilight.

Charlie's MI5 contact had easily tracked Nathaniel Danvers and his team back to Comitán where they had boarded a private flight to Havana. None of them knew why. They doubted Atticus would have sent them on a wild goose chase to Cuba in pursuit of a fictional book of incantations, so there had to be another reason.

Whatever it was, they had little choice but to follow and rescue him. Luckily, Decker had an old buddy from his days in the US Marines who lived in Havana. That meant a warm welcome, good food, and soft beds. He had also promised to use his local knowledge of the island to help them track Atticus and the capstone down.

"Ready for the off?"

She turned and saw Riley. The young Australian was standing in the aisle but leaning casually on the headrest of the seat beside her. As usual, he had brought his wide, toothy smile along with him. Top three buttons of his shirt open, revealing his dog tags and hanging loosely from his tanned wrist, frayed leather surfing bracelets.

She smiled back. "Don't let Captain Mitch see you wandering around on final approach."

"I know," he said with a laugh. "He might put me on a charge."

On the other side of the aisle, Diana huffed out a cynical sigh.

"Di?" Riley asked. "Did you just make a noise like a small rodent breaking wind?"

She put down her book and glared at him. "No, not at all. I agree with you about Mitch."

He furrowed his brow in confusion. "You do?"

"Of course," she said, returning to her book and arching an eyebrow. "What an irritation it is having a responsible, sensible man at the controls of our plane."

"I walked right into that one."

"Yes, you did. Now sit down and buckle up like a good little boy and stop being so silly."

He puffed out his chest. "You think us SAS guys sit down and buckle up?"

She shrugged. "What would your sergeant tell you to do when your plane was coming into land?"

"To sit down and buckle up, of course." He slammed down next to her and reached around for the belt. "That's what I like about you, Di. You're down to earth. You call a spade a spade."

From the cabin, she heard Decker moaning. "Buckle up, Riley!"

"On it, Cap!"

Decker groaned again. "All I wanted was just a..."

"Just a quiet cargo business," Selena called back. "I know. *I know.*"

The American gave a weary laugh. "Okay everyone, we're about to hit the deck."

*

A short drive from the airport and they were pulling up outside Decker's buddy's place in Cojímar. It was modest but beautiful and offered a great sea view. When Decker rang the bell, they noticed the front door was already open. Decker and Selena exchanged a glance, fearing the worst.

Decker poked his head through the gap. "Cade?"

Silence.

"You okay, old buddy?"

"Hey, Mitch!"

Decker blew out a sigh of relief and led the rest of the crew into the small house. He followed the sound of a loud TV set to a back room where they discovered a tall, thin man dressed in a Hawaiian shirt and loud Bermuda shorts.

"Lena, meet Cade Thurman. Cade, meet Lena."

Thurman struggled out of his Ezee Life recliner and wiped a greasy hand on his stained shorts. "Great to meet you, Lena."

Selena eyed the hand for a second, swallowed hard, and took it in hers, shaking it. "Yes, the pleasure is all... mine. I'm sure."

He grinned. "You like fried shrimp?"

"Um, what?"

Decker chuckled. "Do you like fried shrimp?"

"I never…"

"She's crazy about it, Cade," Decker said.

Cade reached around behind the chair and produced a bucket of cold, fried shrimp. Giving the posh English professor a genuine, disarming smile, he said, "What's mine is mine!" Then he belched loudly.

Wafting the stench of stale lager from her face with a slim, pale hand, Selena turned to Decker. "Mitch, are you *sure* Mr. Thurman is the right man for the job?"

"You wanted the best, right?" Cade said.

Selena fixed him in the eye. "Why, of course."

Cade's grin grew wider. "Well… he couldn't make it, so you got me instead!"

Riley and Charlie laughed. Felipe Acosta looked more nervous than amused.

"Ah, another funny one," Diana said. "Great news."

"C'mon guys!" Cade said, indicating the chairs. "Take a load off."

They sat and cracked open some beers. "So," Selena said, wincing at the cheap, sharp lager. "Mitch says you two are old *army* buddies."

Thurman stared at Decker, horrified.

Decker said, "She does it on purpose. She knows we were both marines. Ignore."

Selena sipped more lager and winced again. "Can't blame a gal for trying. Goodness, this beer is *different*."

Cade laughed. "Yeah, I was in the Marines with Mitch. We left around the same time and when he bought his plane and started up Avalon Cargo, I pursued other avenues."

"He means he stole a car and served time in Miami in jail," Decker said.

Thurman gasped. "That is a total lie."

"Was it?"

"Surely. It was a pickup truck."

Diana gasped. "You stole a pickup truck?"

He shrugged. "In my defense, it was *mine*."

"It was your ex's," Decker said.

"Ah, but I *thought* it was mine at the time."

Selena looked at him oddly. "You thought it was yours?"

"Yeah. I thought it was in my name, but it was in my *then*-wife's name. We'd already separated at that time. I went over and picked it up and she called the cops on me. They picked me up on the interstate and she pressed charges, as cool as ice."

"What a babe!" Riley said.

Charlie gave a sympathetic smile. "How kind of her."

"Yeah," Cade said with a fading smile. "She was always a very kind lady." The smile returned and he clapped his hands together. "Anyway, what can I do for you, old buddy? You said you were in some trouble."

"More than a little," Decker said.

"In that case, let's go outside and fire up the barbecue. Three-day-old fried shrimp only goes so far, you know what I'm saying?"

*

They explained their situation over a dinner of grilled steaks and fresh vegetables, and Cade even supplied some half-decent bottles of red and white wine. After dinner, Selena sipped some white wine and watched the Straits of Florida sparkle in the bright Cuban moonlight. After the brutal fighting back in the jungle, it felt good to ease back into a soft chair and enjoy a cold drink. By the looks on the faces of the rest of the crew, she wasn't the only one who felt this way. Decker was lying back on a reclining chair, snoozing with his hat over his face, Charlie and Diana were playing cards, and Riley and Acosta were making headway into two glasses of iced Cuban rum.

Hot sea air blew over their balcony and reminded Selena of long-forgotten summer vacations with her parents. A happy childhood, with everything in the right place. A safe house with a loving mother, good food, and lots of books. A father who brought spontaneous adventure into her life with a mischievous smile.

What a life she had led. Mohenjo-Daro. Angkor Wat. Petra. Chichén Itzá. Knossos. All these amazing archaeological sites and many others all before she was ten. A love of the ancient past ran through her veins in the same blood that ran through her father's veins. Any other life she found impossible to imagine. She closed her eyes and blew out a deep breath, praying her father was all right.

To her left, Diana had grown tired of beating Charlie at poker and threw her hand down. "I'm out, Charlie. For the night."

"Just as I was starting to win!" he said.

She gave him a withering look. "We've played over twenty hands and you only won the third one."

"And now my luck is changing. I feel it in the air."

"Then you play against the air. I'm tired."

As he mumbled to himself and picked up the cards, she hid her smile and took a sip of her wine. It was a Cuban vintage Cade had picked up someplace and tasted good. It reminded her a little of the *alentajo* her parents used to drink with meals at the weekend. She felt a wave of homesickness when she thought about home. Her parents had almost died at the hands of Rakesh Madan during the Shambhala mission, and all because of her involvement in it. For that, she would always feel a pang of terrible guilt.

She raised her glass and made a silent toast to her family's health back in Porto and then took a long sip. Another breeze of hot night air blew across the balcony and rippled through her hair. It felt good. Another memory of warm Portuguese nights with the family. For how much longer she would be able to fly around the world at a moment's notice with the Avalon crew, she had no idea. Sometimes she couldn't imagine any other sort of life. Other times, she wanted to quit the team and fly back to her old life.

"So what's the plan?" Charlie asked, breaking the relaxed silence.

"The plan is we sleep," Cade said. "It's getting late and we have no leads. In the morning, we start looking for your kidnapped dude and the magic keystone."

"That's my *father*, not a kidnapped dude," Selena said. "And it's a capstone, not a keystone. Other than that, you're doing well."

"Thanks, man."

Decker woke from his slumber, removed the hat from his face, and ran a hand through his hair. "I'm beat. I'm calling it a night."

26

Across the city, Tarántula watched the house from the darkness of his car. The old colonial property dated from the 1920s and was an impressive sight in the city center. Set over four floors, with the top three all having balcony access, the bright pink townhouse commanded a beautiful view over the ocean. The boulevard was mostly quiet and parked outside were several brightly colored Buick and Chevrolet convertibles from the 1950s, ubiquitous on the island.

But Tarántula was not in a brightly colored vintage convertible. He was sitting inside a rented black Cadillac Escalade alongside the Mercado brothers and each of them was concentrating on the figure of Professor Salvador Diaz. The old man was pottering around on the top floor of his home, possibly watering plants. It was hard to tell, exactly.

It didn't matter. Whatever he was doing was about to come to a swift and brutal end. It had to be that way. It was what the Snake King had ordered and he had to be obeyed. They had already snatched the English archaeologist, but now he wanted this man, too, and if he had learned one thing, it was never to question the Snake King.

"And this is definitely the correct address?" he asked coolly.

"Yes, boss," Carlos said. "Triple checked."

"And I asked at the local store just down the road," Miguel said. "Old couple. They were very helpful. They confirmed this is his address."

"How helpful were they?" Tarántula asked. "Not helpful enough to give the police your description?"

"Not that helpful, boss. They're now both lying dead in the back room."

"Good, very good," Tarántula purred. "We cannot fail *el rey serpiente*. The Snake King is not known for his forgiving nature."

The Mercados shared another quiet look. Raised in a strict Catholic family, neither brother held any stock in the idea of ancient Maya gods meting out divine retribution. All they cared about was the large amount of gold they had been promised by Tarántula on completion of this job. Then they would quietly slip away to a beach they knew in Costa Rica. Buy a bar and live out their lives surrounded by beautiful local women in awe of their wealth and power. That was all the Mercado brothers cared about anymore.

"All right." Tarántula glanced at his Rolex Daytona. "It's time. Take him."

Carlos and Miguel Mercado didn't have to look at each other. They each popped open their door and climbed out of the Escalade. Business as usual. A sniff and a sigh. Eyes swiveling for cops. A quick pat of the jacket to make sure the *cuete* was in place, all locked and loaded and ready for action.

Carlos brushed his knuckles on his jawline as they crossed the street. Miguel pulled a *cohiba* cigarette from a fresh pack he had stolen from the tobacconists he had just murdered. He offered one to his older brother who waved it away. Miguel lit the cigarette and blew the fragrant smoke out into the humid night air. Of all the *dichos* or sayings that he knew, *poco a poco se andra lejos*. Little by little, one goes far, was the one he believed in most.

Once just two boys from the world's largest slum in

Nezo-Chalco-Itza, today they had seen and done it all. Now, after the prospect of endless years in an American maximum-security prison, they were on the cusp of not only retiring as free, wealthy men but also getting the chance to wipe out millions of Americans. Who knew revenge could be so sweet? Just take it one step at a time, Mico, his inner voice told him. One small step at a time, and you will create great things for yourself. You will have everything you ever wanted.

Carlos was a step ahead of him, walking to the front door and stepping up into the shadows. The big broad-backed Mexican was out of sight now, beneath the colonial-style portico. He rang the bell, sniffed, and turned to his baby brother. "Let's get this over with. Nice and fast and quiet. Get him back to the car and then we can get out of here."

"Agreed."

Casually, as if he was pulling a wallet from his pocket, he drew a Jericho 941 from a holster under his jacket. Gun controls in both Mexico and Cuba were some of the strictest in the world, but getting hold of a weapon like this, or bringing it into Havana presented little problem. At least, not when you owned the people Tarántula owned, and this was further facilitated by the use of the big man's impressive private jet.

Miguel flicked his cigarette onto the sidewalk and pulled his own weapon, a neat Beretta 92. He exhaled the smoke and turned to keep the gun out of sight. Then, the door opened.

"Si?"

"Professor Diaz?" Carlos asked.

"Yes, that's me. How can I help?"

Carlos raised the gun and stepped forward. It happened lightning fast. The muzzle was now pushed into the man's forehead and Carlos was inside the hall, pushing him back out of sight. Miguel turned and checked no one had seen, then followed his brother inside and closed the door behind him.

"What is this?" Diaz said, his voice trembling. "I have nothing of value!"

"That's where you are very wrong," Carlos said, pistol-whipping the man and knocking him clean out. He collapsed down onto an antique runner on his floorboards. "Very wrong indeed."

"You think he's all right?" Miguel asked.

"He's fine. Check the street is clear then bring the Escalade up to the sidewalk. I'll pick him up and take him out to the car."

When his brother disappeared out of the front door, Carlos slipped his gun into his holster and reached down and heaved the unconscious man into a fireman's lift. Then, when his brother told him the coast was clear from outside near the Cadillac, he walked briskly down the path with the professor and tumbled his body into the back of the SUV. He slammed the rear door shut and climbed into the front. Miguel was already at the wheel.

"Good," Tarántula said. "You have done well."

27

Diana sipped her coffee and opened the newspaper she had just bought at the local store. It was a bright, warm morning and the walk had been quiet and relaxing. Like the rest of the Avalon crew, the thought of Atticus's kidnapping was weighing down heavily on her, so she followed her mother's favorite advice and took a good, long walk to clear her mind and get some perspective.

Sitting in a beam of relaxing sunshine at Cade's patio table in his back yard, she took another sip of the coffee and started to go through the newspaper. It relaxed her further and took her mind away from the mission. But not for long. When she opened the front cover and looked inside, she saw a picture of a townhouse somewhere in Havana and, inset, a grainy black and white portrait photograph of an old, wiry man with a gray beard.

She read the story with interest and then said, "You get many kidnappings in Cuba?"

"Not at all," Cade said. "It's not Mexico."

"In that case, I might have an idea why Danvers came here."

Selena said, "You do?"

"Sure." Diana folded her copy of *Granma* down and peered at Selena over the top of it. "It says in here that there was a kidnapping in the city last night."

"Are you certain?" Selena asked.

She nodded. "It's written in Spanish, not Portuguese, but I am fluent in Spanish. It's clear enough. It says that last night, there was a break-in at the address of a Professor Salvador Diaz over in *Habana Vieja*."

"The Old Town," Cade said, scraping some butter over his toast. "It's not far from here, just over the Canal de Entrada. You drove through it last night to get here."

"Interesting," Decker said. "Maybe this might speed things up a bit."

Charlie sipped his freshly ground coffee and stretched his arms. "What else does it say?"

Diana dipped her head back into the newspaper. "Last night Professor Diaz was reported missing by his niece. She was supposed to be meeting him for a late dinner but when she got to his address she found the door open and signs of a struggle in the hallway. She reported it to the Havana Police Department straight away and they immediately traveled to the property, which they searched. They found no sign of him. Neighbors reported that they saw suspicious-looking men parked outside his house."

"Suspicious how?" Charlie asked. "Slightly suspicious, or like Riley?"

Riley laughed. "You're a really funny bloke, Charlie."

"Would police normally respond so fast?" Decker asked.

Cade shook his head. "I wouldn't have thought so. Not unless he was someone pretty important."

"He was," Diana said. "The report ends by saying that he was the head of the Physics Faculty at the University of Havana, specializing in weather modification and a high-ranking member of the Communist Party of Cuba."

"*Muy importante*," Cade said with a chuckle, then took a large bite of his toast.

"Does it say anything else?" Selena asked. "What sort of car it was, for example?"

"A black SUV," she said. "American. One of the neighbors said it might have been an Escalade. That's it."

"Is it enough to go on?" Decker asked.

"Maybe," Charlie said. "My guys at MI5 aren't magicians though. Having said that, they might be able to get hold of some satellite recon. Cuba is pretty heavily covered. Always has been, for all the obvious historical and strategic reasons."

"It's all we have," Diana said.

Riley was lighting the biggest cigar any of them had ever seen. He leaned back on his chair and sucked on the enormous Partagas. Blowing out a big puff of blue smoke, he smiled broadly. "I predict a successful few hours here in Cuba."

"Oh yeah?" Selena said.

Acosta waved the smoke away, coughing.

"Yeah," Riley said. "The satellite data from Charlie's mates will show us where they took old Diaz, and then we'll go and get him and Atticus back before retrieving the capstone."

"You think it's going to be that easy?" Cade said.

The Australian shrugged and grinned and sucked on the cigar again. "Let's just say, I can feel our plan coming together."

28

The Snake King grabbed a fistful of the vinyl tarp covering the Stormbringer but hesitated before wrenching it away. The last time he had stared into its polished surfaces, back in the caves of Xibalba in the Lacandon Jungle, he had been given a vision of the future which had terrifyingly come almost perfectly true. Now, having had time to think about this ancient power more carefully, he grew nervous about whether or not he was truly ready to know more of what the future held.

He gazed around at his men, standing in a semi-circle with their hands on their weapons in the enormous space. The warehouse was down on the docks near the ferry terminals and had belonged to a tobacco packing company up until a few weeks ago. Waiting for a commercial tenant, the place was empty and eerie but gave the Snake King all the space and privacy he needed.

He smoothly pulled off the tarp and beheld the swirling patterns in wonder.

"You know how this works?"

Professor Salvador Diaz looked at his captors with disgust. The man in the green jade mask covered in snakes was particularly unsettling, but he stood his ground. "Even if I did, I would never tell you."

The Snake King gave a sad smile, only partly visible through the slit in the jade mask. "I thought this might be your response. This is why I had some of my men take your niece as well."

Diaz jumped from his chair and stared at him with a burning hatred. "No! No one would do something so evil!"

"Think again, old man," the Snake King said. He turned to Carlos Mercado. "Show him your phone."

Carlos stepped forward and held out his phone, allowing the old man to see the screen. When he saw it, he recoiled in horror. There, on the tiny screen of the cell phone, he saw a picture of his young niece, gagged and bound and scared out of her mind. Two men he had never seen before were smiling into the camera. They each wore bandanas and were holding flick knives.

"You bastards!"

Carlos laughed and put the phone back in his pocket.

The Snake King's face remained calm and mild. "An understandable reaction. I take no offense. You will, however, now see more clearly why it is so imperative that you give me what I want and assist me with this device."

"You'll have to comply," said Atticus, hands tied behind his back. "They're maniacs."

Diaz listened to the words of the old English professor and started to pale. "Please, don't harm her! She is only young. Just twenty-three. She is getting married in a few months. Let her be, I beg you."

"Her welfare is entirely in your hands, Professor Diaz. Help me activate and control this device and I will contact the team holding her and have her released. Refuse, and I will have her head deposited on your front lawn."

Diaz looked like he was going to be sick. He raised a hand to his mouth to hold back the vomit and worked hard to shake the image from his mind. "I will do as you ask," he said at last. "Anything to save young Cristina."

"You are a smart man, Salvador," the Snake King said, giving the old man's cheek a few disrespectful pats. "I knew eventually you would come to the sensible position and give me what I want."

The old man buckled, dropped to his knees, and began examining the capstone. He was intrigued by the smoky patterns in the metal and began to feel strange sensations as he stared into it. Pulling back before he was overwhelmed, he soon found his way to the enigmatic pyramid's base.

"Interesting," he muttered, picking up the chipped ohmmeter his captors had given to him and taking some measurements. "Very interesting."

"What is it?' the Snake King barked. "What do you see?"

Diaz stopped what he was doing and twisted his neck around to look up at him. "Where did you get this device?"

"That is none of your concern. You are here to make it work. That's all."

Diaz sighed. "But something's not right here."

Behind him, Carlos Mercado said, "I think I heard something outside."

"Then check it out, amigo," said Tarántula. "Now."

"Si."

The Snake King looked at Diaz. "What do you mean when you say something is not right, old man?"

"First, I cannot identify this particular metal. It seems to be silver and yet it's not. It shares certain similarities with copper, but it is not copper. The mechanism inside the device seems at once both ancient and modern. It vexes me."

"Do you understand how it works or not?" the Snake King said. "My patience is running low."

Diaz looked back to the capstone and crouched down again. Dipping his head to study the base one more time, he mumbled what sounded like a positive affirmation. "Interesting... intriguing."

The Snake King's eyes blinked behind the mask.

"What does that mean, Professor Diaz?"

"It's all very odd, but I think I can see through it to the basics. It appears to be some sort of crude ferromagnetic apparatus for producing a natural waveguide."

"Like a conductor?"

"Not exactly," Diaz said. "There is a difference between a conductor and a waveguide."

"Explain."

Diaz was still exploring the mechanism deep inside the capstone's interior. "A waveguide is any structure or device which guides waves."

"Are you trying to be funny?" the Snake King said. "Do I need to remind you that one phone call to my associates and your niece is dead?"

"I am not trying to be funny!" Diaz said hurriedly. "I am answering your question."

"Then get on with it."

"Very well...as I said, a waveguide is a device that guides waves. These could be sound waves or radio waves or electromagnetic waves. A waveguide is designed to channel and focus and transmit the waves in a particular direction while retaining as much of the original energy as possible. The entire planet is a kind of natural waveguide, formed by the relative positions of the earth's surface and the ionosphere. It resonates at 7.83 Hz, or what we call the Schumann Resonance. These waves can be channeled and used for several purposes."

"I am not a scientist, Professor Diaz."

"Let me give you an example. The HAARP facility in Alaska can be utilized to cause tropical cyclones anywhere in the world."

The Snake King laughed. "Conspiracy theory drivel."

Diaz crawled out from beneath the capstone and got to his feet. "You can tell yourself that if it helps you sleep at night, but I am telling you what I know to be true.

HAARP can use waveguides to direct specially designed tandem-array waves of electromagnetic energy into the ionosphere and then aim them wherever is required. This way, tropical cyclones or hurricanes can be formed wherever and whenever is desired."

The man behind the mask blinked, his deranged mind suddenly whirring with possibilities. "I don't believe it."

"And yet you have kidnapped a physicist specializing in weather modification. Why do so, if you do not want to hear what I have to say?"

The Snake King thought it over. "You're not lying, then?"

"No, I am not lying. Moreover, I believe this device you have here is very similar to the one used at the HAARP facility, with one very important exception."

"And what might that be?"

"I believe it is much more powerful."

The Snake King held his surprise in check. "How so?"

"Waveguides rely on hollow metallic conductors. Silver is the best conductor we know of, and yet this device is made from something else entirely. I have already run a simple conductivity test with the ohmmeter and it is showing interesting results. Whatever metallic substance this metal is, it has a conductivity several orders of magnitude greater than even silver."

"How much more powerful?"

"At least a thousand times."

The other men fell silent, suddenly interested in what he had to say.

"Say that again, old man," said the Snake King. "Slowly."

"I said the metallic substance that this device is made from is at least a thousand times better at conducting electricity than silver. I have seen nothing like it throughout my entire career. I believe when activated it will channel unimaginable quantities of energy into the atmosphere." He scratched his head. "I just wish I knew more about this metal."

"I call it *divinium*," the Snake King said. "Metal of the gods."

Diaz took a cautious step away from the man in front of him. "Whatever you call it, it must be handled with care. If directed into the ionosphere, this could create a force more powerful than dozens of hurricanes all hitting at the same time."

"It's that powerful?"

"Easily, and much more so if it can increase and direct natural waveguides existing in the planet's crust. If it is capable of amplifying these waves, it could be truly devastating. You do indeed have in your hands some sort of god device."

"Yes, the power of the gods!" he said. "Can you operate it?"

"I believe so. The removal of this idol on the top would activate it initially, and then there are some crude controls beneath which regulate the power."

"Good, very good."

Carlos Mercado ran back into the large warehouse space. "We've got company."

"Who?" Tarántula asked.

"Looks like the same ones as before."

"The Avalon crew?"

Carlos nodded. "They took a shot at me! They're heading this way!"

"How the hell did they survive?" Tarántula said.

"I don't know. Maybe we could ask them when they get in here, guns blazing?"

"Don't be a smart mouth, Carlos. I should kill you where you stand for not making sure they died back there when I told you to. Now you have another chance. Kill them!"

"Wait!" the Snake King snapped. "Tarántula and Novarro will come with me. We will take the capstone and the hostages and get to the jet. Diablo and the Mercado brothers will keep the Avalon crew busy and give us time to get away. Now, go!"

29

Decker had fired the shot at Carlos Mercado when he stepped outside the warehouse. He missed and the Mexican gangster scrambled back inside without returning fire. He turned to the rest of the crew who were standing around their two vehicles – Cade's personal car and their hired SUV, guns in hand. "We have to go in!"

"No, wait!" Riley was looking along the side of the warehouse. "Looks like they're splitting up. I see an Escalade taking off and heading south but they've left some dudes behind to hold us back."

Charlie took a shot at the Cadillac, a puff of white smoke from his gun drifted up lazily into the hot air as the round pinged off a nearby road sign. "Missed."

"They're stopping us from taking off after the Caddy!" Cade said.

"Which is already long gone…" mumbled Diana.

"No, it's not," Decker said. "I'll stay here with Cade and Lena and deal with the goons inside the warehouse. Riley, you take our SUV and get after the Escalade."

"Got it."

"What about you?" Diana asked.

"As I said, we'll try and take these guys out," he said with a shrug. "It's all we can do."

"What if they take off?"

"We have my car!" Cade said.

Diana looked at the old Buick and frowned. "Really?"

"Hey, she's solid gold!"

"If you say so…"

Decker watched his friends climb into their hired SUV

and drive south of the warehouse, swerving out onto the main road and giving pursuit of the fleeing Escalade. Then the shooting stopped.

"What are they playing at?"

Before anyone answered, a black Mercedes ML350 burst out of the large hangar-sized door and raced straight toward them.

"Holy crap!" Cade said. "They're heading for my car!"

Decker calmly rested his arms on the Buick's roof and peeled off a few rounds, aiming straight for the driver's half of the windshield. The rounds punctured the glass and forced the driver to duck and swerve at the very last minute. The chunky black Mercedes blew past them with inches to spare and swerved out of the parking lot.

"Now they're getting away too!" Selena said. "Did anyone see if Dad was in there?"

"Funnily enough," Cade said, crawling up off the asphalt, "No. You?"

"No!"

"Talk later," Decker said. "Now, action."

Decker swung open the door of Cade's 1953 Buick Special and turned the ignition key as the other piled in. The Nailhead V8 roared to life as he stamped on the pedal and the car surged forward. Selena was gripping the seat, a string of curses fluttering from her lips. Up ahead, the Mercedes ML350 was clearing the industrial park and opening a wide lead on them.

"We're going awfully fast, Mitch!"

Decker pushed the vintage Buick harder and steered out of the park onto the road in a screech of squealing tires. "That's sort of how you catch up with people."

"Point taken."

The black Merc was stretching away now, turning off San Pedro and disappearing into the labyrinthine streets of the Old Town. Decker spun the wheel hard to the left and swerved onto a side street called Sol. The Merc was ahead of them but already making a hard right out of sight.

"You're losing them!" she said. "Maybe if your friend had bought a car from this century we might stand a better chance!"

"This car is a classic!" Cade protested. "Right, Mitch?"

"Sure is." He gave the steering wheel a loving tap. "It's old school. Beautiful. Great transmission, quality rear differential. This is a car to fall in love with, made back when they knew how to build cars."

"This again..." Selena mumbled.

"And what is *that* supposed to mean?"

"Sounds like you love this old car more than the Avalon."

Decker swerved off Oficios and onto Muralla, narrowly avoiding a dangerous collision with a delivery truck. "Now, let's not be silly. This car is beautiful, but the Avalon is pure art."

Selena rolled her eyes and rolled down the window. "I'm going to let you quietly undress your airplane in your mind while I try and stop these maniacs from taking my father away!"

"Take it easy!" Decker said. "Your Dad might be in there!"

"I'm aiming for the tires!"

She fired on the Mercedes as it entered a broad plaza busy with tourists. Hearing the report of the pistol, everyone in the square bolted for safety, running into cafés and boutiques and restaurants and alleys. Decker screeched into the Plaza Vieja and was forced to steer hard to avoid the last few people still in the ancient public square.

"You have a good clear shot!" he called out.

"Maybe I might have if you could keep this old heap

steady for more than a few seconds."

"Hey!" Cade said.

Decker laughed. "And I love you too, darling…"

She fired again but missed. The Mercedes was already across the plaza and vanishing into another maze of backstreets in the city's historic district. Then, Carlos and Miguel Mercado appeared, each leaning out of his window on either side of the Merc with Diablo at the wheel. Each one was holding a compact machine pistol.

"Incoming, Mitch!"

Decker saw the two men holding the guns a second before they opened fire and swerved hard to avoid the rounds. Bullets raked into the tiled ground as the American skidded around the fenced-off fountain in the center of the plaza. The old Buick tipped up onto its two left wheels and Decker thought they were going to tip over, but he managed to bring the car safely back to earth with a grinding crunch of the seventy-year-old suspension.

"Sorry Cade…" he mumbled.

"That's going to hurt," said his old friend.

"Right!" Selena called out. "Go right! They're going north."

"Damn it all," Decker muttered. "This is turning into another hot mess."

"I'm taking another shot!" Selena said.

She clicked a new mag into the firearm receiver and raised the gun into the aim. Squinting down the length of the barrel at the sight, she gently squeezed the trigger and fired off a single round at the Mercedes. The round missed its mark, which was to take out one of the tires and buried itself in some plaster in a nearby building.

Decker spoke without taking his eyes off the road. "So, your aim's getting better."

The men fired back and hit their front tire. This time,

their faster speed meant Decker was unable to control the car. As the rubber flew off the tire and spun out into the street, the car swerved violently to the right and plowed into a sidewalk café.

"Brace!" he yelled.

Slowed by the heavy iron tables and chairs, the car came to a stop when it ground along the side of the café and then crashed into a perpendicular wall.

"Shit, my car!" Cade said.

"We lost them, Mitch!"

He put an arm around her. "I know. I'm so sorry."

"They still have Dad!"

"I know, damn it! I can't believe we lost them! I need a second here." Decker was trying to clear his head when Selena's phone rang.

She looked down at the screen. "It's Diana..." she said and took the call. After a long tense silence, she thanked her old friend and hung up. Paler now, and trembling, she looked up, first at Cade and then over to Decker.

"She said they got away."

"Damn it!" said Decker.

"Don't worry about it," Cade said. "I have some buddies who were CIA. They might be able to help with flight plans."

"That's something, at least," said Decker.

Selena was still paling. "That's not all. She said the Snake King's men fired on the SUV and forced it into a roll. She told me Charlie was knocked out and wouldn't come around. They're taking him to a hospital right now."

Decker and Cade exchanged a grim look.

"Shit," Cade said. "Not good news."

"He'll be fine," said Decker. "Which hospital?"

"Hermanos Ameijeiras," she said.

"That's good," Cade said. "It's a good, modern hospital. In Barrio San Lazaro."

"How quickly can we be there?" Selena asked.

"With traffic, twenty minutes."

Decker had already got outside and opened the trunk. "Then let's get this tire fixed and get over there. Right now this whole mission feels like it's falling apart and it's about time we started to pull it back together."

"I hope Charlie's all right," Selena said.

Decker slid the jack under the chassis. "He'll be fine. He's built like a brick outhouse."

"I hope you're right."

"I am, and you two are heavy, so get out and let me jack this baby up. The quicker we get a new tire on her, the quicker we're where we need to be."

30

Decker opened his eyes to a white room filled with sunshine. Exhausted from the chase, and the long wait to see if Charlie would be discharged from the hospital, they were all feeling bruised and hurt. He had presumed his old friend would be conscious by the time he got to the hospital and all would be well. That hadn't happened. When they got there, a grim-faced Diana explained what the doctors had already told her: Charlie had suffered a severe head injury and was still unconscious. There was talk of comas. He would have to stay in overnight.

Now, Decker yawned and stretched his arms. The sun in the room grew brighter. They had forgotten to close the blinds last night and now the sunlight streaked across the room, projecting slats of shadow on the wall at the end of the bed. He yawned and pulled himself up until his back was leaning on the headboard. Outside, the morning was already underway in Havana but there was no sign of Selena except a crumpled pillow beside him and the sound of a shower running in the en suite bathroom.

He yawned once again and contemplated the mission. He'd had no time to indulge in actual thinking since that dreamy afternoon in the convent back in Guanajuato. Turning to his right, he cast his eye over the view outside Cade's house, available to enjoy through the slats of the open Venetian blinds hanging down over the window.

It was spectacular. The house was on the Via de la Mar, set just behind a line of low sand dunes. Beyond those, the *playas del este* were a long strip of bright gold sand punctuated with coconut palms and royal palms and thatched beach huts. Behind this, a strong ribbon of turquoise sparkled in the sun. This was the Straits of Florida, and like most days, it was buzzing with swimmers and jet skiers and windsurfers. Lively Spanish floated on the warm morning air. Laughter and shouts of joy. Children played with their parents in the warm sand. For a moment, Decker almost felt like he was on vacation.

He shifted in the sheets, comfortable and naked. He just slept better that way, he mused. Then, his thoughts returned to contemplating the mission. The revelation that Professor Nathaniel Danvers was suffering from the mother of all Napoleon complexes had been a bitter blow to the crew, but they had taken it in their stride. Even Diana had risen to some of the hard physical challenges the mission had presented.

The en suite door opened to reveal a semi-naked Selena Moore. She was wrapping a towel around herself as she stepped into the bedroom and flashed Decker a smile.

"Even more beautiful than the beach," he said with a twinkle of his eye.

She leaned forward and began brushing her wet hair. "Flattery will get you everywhere."

"That's what I was hoping. Good shower?"

"You can say that again. Back in the Lacandon Jungle, I was starting to think I'd never be clean again."

He laughed. "I know how you feel. Too bad I was too exhausted for one last night."

"You weren't *that* exhausted," she said with a wicked grin.

"You can talk! And there was I, thinking you were an up-market lady."

She flicked her hair back and walked over to her clothes on the chair. "Please Captain Decker, you'll make me blush."

He laughed but said nothing. Just relaxed into the sheets and enjoyed the moment. Then Diana knocked on the door.

"Come in!" Selena said.

"It's just me," she said. "I just got a call from the hospital. They say Charlie regained consciousness in the night and he's okay."

"Thank heavens for that!' Selena said. "I was worried sick."

"Any word on when he's getting discharged?" asked Decker. "Don't forget, we still have to rescue Atticus and Professor Diaz, not to mention secure the capstone. We might have to do the rest of the mission without him."

"I don't think this will be necessary," Diana said. "They say he can come home today, so I guess that means here."

Decker grinned. "Or the Avalon, right?"

Diana smiled and left the room, closing the door behind her.

"So, what's next?" Selena asked.

"We pick up Charlie and get him out of there. Then, it gets tougher. Danvers is still holding your father and Professor Diaz hostage, for one thing. Think about Diaz for a second. He's a renowned physicist and engineer specializing in waveguide technology and directed energy weapons. This much we definitely know. From this, it's easy to work out he needs this man to operate the Stormbringer."

Selena was doing up her jeans and reaching for a top. "The problem is, how do we know where he intends to use the device?"

"To know that, we have to wait and see if Cade's CIA buddies can tell us."

They finished getting dressed and stepped out onto the patio where Cade was already rustling up a breakfast of pancakes and syrup. "You guys sleep well?"

"Not really, Mr. Thurman," Selena said. "You might remember, that not only was an old friend of mine hospitalized but also that my father was kidnapped by a lunatic who thinks he's a Maya king with the divine right to destroy the world with a doomsday device."

"And you don't hear *that* every day," Riley said, mouth full of pancake.

"Sorry," Cade said. "Just being polite."

"Of course, you were," Selena said. "I apologize. It's just that after yesterday and the warehouse and everything, I really thought we were going to get Dad back. I'm still reeling from that a bit, I think."

"No problemo," Cade said. "Coffee?"

She nodded and he poured out another cup. "I just wish we were doing something, *anything*, to get Dad back. I feel like I'm letting him down. I mean, he's in the clutches of this Danvers man and I'm just sitting here drinking coffee."

"And eating pancakes covered in syrup," Riley said.

"Thank you," she said, pushing the plate away. "Suddenly, I'm not hungry anymore."

Acosta stepped out of the room with his phone in his hand. He saw the pile of fresh pancakes and his eyes widened. "Sabroso!"

"Any news about Danvers?" Decker asked Cade. "Your CIA friends come through for us?"

"Sure," Cade said nonchalantly. "He flew out of Havana a few hours ago."

Selena sat up on her chair, a nervous look in her eyes. "Destination?"

"Miami." Cade swallowed the last of his coffee and belched loudly. "Which is my hometown. I can't wait to show you guys around."

Selena waved the foul air away from her face with a

frown. "Thanks ever so much."

"Welcome."

Decker set his coffee cup down and pushed back from the table. "Let's pick up Charlie and get to the airport as fast as we can. We can be in Miami around an hour after take-off."

31

Miami Beach, Florida

Tarántula didn't like the look in the Snake King's eyes. The man from Acapulco was a hardened gang boss and there was nothing imaginable he had not seen or done. On his journey from the backstreets of Progreso to the luxury condominiums of Cancún, he had met every kind of man and woman and thought he had nothing new to learn. And yet this man, this Danvers, had a crazed look in his eye he had never seen before.

He lit a long Cuban cigar and leaned back on his recliner, studying the Canadian academic a little more closely, in the way he might examine an ant crawling around the inside of an upturned glass. They were sitting on the sun deck of the *Holcan*, the Snake King's luxury yacht, moored in the Miami Beach Marina. At any other time, the atmosphere would be calm, relaxing. A good time to chill out and let the gentle bobbing of the yacht lull you into a soft, warm doze.

But no, not now.

Now, the Snake King had removed the tarp and was staring into the strange swirling metal once again, desperately mumbling to himself as he tried to see another snippet from the future.

"Why is it not working?" he mumbled. "Why are the gods denying me?"

Tarántula noticed a look of skepticism on the faces of his two most loyal lieutenants, Carlos and Miguel

Mercado. The older of the two seemed more than skeptical. He looked like he wanted to kill the Snake King and throw his dead body overboard. But then, that was how he looked at everyone. More interesting was the look on the faces of the two kidnapped academics.

"You think the Snake King cannot read the future, huh?" he said to Atticus.

"I think he is quite insane," Atticus said.

The Snake King was out of earshot at the end of the deck, still staring into the metal.

"He says he saw the future once before, old man. Back in the cave."

"He saw nothing of the sort," Atticus said. "As I say, he is out of his mind and so are you for following him."

"Maybe you should stop wagging your tongue before I cut it out?" Tarántula said coolly. To emphasize the point, he pulled an old Mexican switchblade from his pocket and opened it up with a slick metallic click. The polished steel and ivory handle glinted in the sun. "You agree?"

Atticus said nothing.

"Why are you doing this?" Salvador Diaz said. "Just… why?"

"Ah!" called out the Snake King. "I am beginning to see again!"

He was crouched down close to the capstone, leaning into its strange surface only inches away and hyperventilating with excitement. "I see the future again! Your friends are on their way here… I see them, they are walking to the yacht."

Tarántula and the Mercado brothers exchanged a look and readied their weapons. Novarro and Diablo flicked cigarettes into the water. "If they are, then they are dead," Diablo said.

"We must work faster," the Snake King said.

"Professor Diaz, I require your services."

The old man hesitated but moved when Miguel Mercado pushed the muzzle of his gun up against his temple. "Move, you old fool."

Diaz made his way over to the other side of the sun deck. "What do you want?"

"You will activate the device."

"Are you insane? Here? In Miami Beach?"

The Snake King stared at him with dead eyes. "Miguel, give Sanchez a call. Tell him he can have his fun with the Professor's niece, with my compliments."

"No! Please!"

"Then make the device work."

Diaz crumbled and walked over to the capstone, a broken man. "I will do as you ask, but I might need help. There are some inscriptions on here which I cannot understand."

The Snake King turned to Atticus, staring at him through his mask. "Do it."

"I will not!" Atticus said.

The response was instant. The Snake King looked at Diablo. No words were necessary. Diablo padded over to the old archaeologist and punched him in the face, knocking him back into his seat. The blow hurt like hell and made his head spin. Atticus knew further resistance was futile. If he failed to comply, Danvers would escalate from simply thuggery and make the same threat against poor Diaz's niece. He sighed, got up from his chair, and walked over to the capstone. Giving Diaz a sympathetic look, he began to work on the inscription.

"I can read this," he said. "It's telling us to remove the Huracan idol on top of the capstone if we want to operate it properly, or at least to its maximum potential. There are some other instructions here which I think relate to some of the levers inside the mechanism."

"Then get to work!" the Snake King said. "Or your niece is dead, Professor Diaz!"

With the Mercados' laughter in the air, Diaz dropped to his knees and began to operate the crude magnetron. The device buzzed and hummed and began to glow a bright reddish gold, just as it had back in the cave. When Diaz got to his feet, Carlos Mercado pulled him out of the way and gave the Snake King the room he needed to operate the Stormbringer.

Slowly the device grew in power. Then, a burst of energy ripped up from the center of the capstone and shot into the air. Pelicans screeched and flapped away. The yacht rocked back and forth violently as gray clouds began to form in the blue sky above them.

Tarántula made the sign of the cross and took a step back. "Dios mío!"

The Snake King laughed and watched the flow of energy grow in power. Now, a full storm was already building over Miami Beach. Confused beachgoers were packing up and heading back to their cars as the wind grew in strength. Smaller boats on the marina thrashed violently up and down as the water frothed and bubbled beneath them. The clouds swirled and the storm grew ever more powerful.

"It's turning into a hurricane!" Atticus screamed. "For God's sake turn it off!"

"Silence!" the Snake King yelled. "This is the will of Huracan!"

The wind tore at palm trees, biting at them and then ripping them from the ground. In the marina, several of the yachts were ripped to pieces, their masts were torn out of the decks. Others were tipped over and capsized. Somewhere in the distance, the sound of sirens pierced through the noise of the raging storm and wrapping around all of the chaos, the maniacal sound of the Snake

King's laughter.

Then it stopped when he positioned the carved head of Huracan over the hole at the capstone's center and everything crashed into silence. The energy beam collapsed and the clouds began to dissipate.

"My God!" Diaz said. "This is the work of the devil!"

"And yet I used only a tiny fraction of its power," the Snake King said. "Just think what full power will do! Tarántula, I have decided to change the target of my next strike. Miami is not impressive enough. I want to make a much bigger impression when I strike. Tell the men to prepare the jet for flight. We leave immediately."

32

"Miami Beach Marina." Cade jutted his chin at the yachts bobbing up and down on the sparkling water. Moments earlier, the sky had been a swirling maelstrom of storm clouds and a fierce wind had battered the coast, but now it was once again a normal summer's day. Local news and the internet were abuzz with intrigue and speculation about what had happened, but no one on the Avalon crew needed two guesses to know the truth.

They had just exited their hire car and were walking down a paved slope on the southwestern tip of the South Beach district. Felipe Acosta and Diana had volunteered to stay back at the hotel with a shaken and dazed Charlie Valentine, but Decker had assessed that the remaining crew would be enough to get on the yacht and do what they had to do.

Cade took in a deep breath of sea air and sighed as he took in the damage inflicted by the mini-hurricane. "It's one of the most popular marinas in town, and with the closest mooring to the ocean. Now it looks like they have some rebuilding work to do."

Selena watched as an ambulance parked up at the far end of the marina. Two paramedics got out and ran down a jetty toward a freshly battered yacht. On the far side of the marina, several people were clinging to the hulls of some upturned boats. She took in the billions of dollars' worth of luxury vessels moored up on the Meloy Channel. Further south, a large white cruise ship had sailed into view from the northern shore of Dodge Island and was making its way out to sea along Government Cut.

"Where did your CIA buddy say the *Holcan* was moored?" Decker asked.

"It's one of the more expensive moorings," Cade said. "We're almost there now." He pointed to a white-painted metal gate leading down to a jetty, flanked by palm trees. "It must be behind this blue one, the *Reina*.

This was good luck. The *Holcan* was a hefty Tri-Deck and they could already see its marine radar array protruding above the *Reina*, a large Persian blue flybridge moored just in front of their target yacht. They moved toward it with their weapons concealed inside their jackets, led by Cade in his creased Raffia straw hat and Ray-Ban shades. To their left, an old man heaved a marlin up out of a modest fishing boat and gave them a cheery wave as they passed.

"I hope everyone's ready for a lively discussion," Decker said.

As they passed the *Reina*'s bow, Selena looked up and saw a handful of men milling around in the pilothouse. On the deck above it, one lone figure was standing in the sky lounge. She'd bet the farm it was Danvers, the self-styled Snake King. He was looking away from the marina and out across Government Cut and the Norwegian cruise ship.

"Time to party, kids," Riley said. "Know where your guns are."

The four of them continued toward the *Holcan*, Cade in the lead and followed by Decker and Riley with Selena at the rear.

Noting the absence of guards on the jetty around the yacht, Decker said, "No one to welcome us at the front door?"

"How rude," said Selena.

"Don't let a good opportunity go to waste, right?" Riley said with a grin. "Up we go."

Cade was up the gangway and on the yacht in seconds. Riley was two steps behind him, gun drawn and ready for action. Decker and Selena were on board a second later, reaching for their guns and scanning the deck for any more of the Snake King's small army.

Selena didn't have to look far. Two men turned a corner at the stern end of the deck, walking slowly in casual conversation until one looked up and saw them. They reached for the weapons but Riley was already running toward them. The tall Australian shoulder-barged one straight over the rail and into the sea and then turned and delivered a bone-crunching headbutt into the face of the other, collapsing his nose and sending him crashing to the deck in a spray of blood.

"Fuck, that hurt!" he called out, rubbing his forehead. "I forget how much that hurt!"

"Riley!" Selena cried out. She was standing at his side now, along with Cade and Decker. "Finish the job, please."

"Sure thing, boss."

The punch was a big, ugly shield of seasoned knuckles driven into the man's temple and knocked him out, hard and cold. He slid down into the pool of blood formed by his smashed nose. Riley disarmed him and tossed the weapon out into the water where the other man was splashing around and calling out, trying to alert the others to the invasion.

They heard shouting on the deck above them and then a loud, ear-piercing siren. Decker thought it sounded like a standard high-bilge-water alarm, but now it was being used to alert the guards on board to their presence on the yacht. Chaos kicked in like a rocket booster.

"We need to split up," Decker said. "I'll take Riley and go to the stern. We'll try and find Atticus and Diaz. Cade, you take Selena and try and find the capstone."

Cade gave a two-fingered salute, his fingers brushing against the rim of his straw hat. "Sir, yes sir!"

"Let's move!" Decker said.

Selena watched the former marine lead Riley down the deck and disappear out of sight at the stern. Alone with Cade, she wasn't sure where to start looking for the Stormbringer.

"Where do you think the bastard is keeping it?" Cade said.

"I have no idea," she said with a sigh. "It could be anywhere."

"But inside is a good bet, right?

She nodded and followed Cade into a large seating area full of soft leather couches and potted palms. Then, a man with a long black ponytail burst into the room. He was already gripping a gun, and now he leveled it at them and prepared to fire. Selena knew what she had to do, and brought her gun up but it was too late. Cade fired first and shot him clean through the head. A sickening spray of blood and bone exploded in the air as the man tumbled down onto the coffee-colored carpet.

"Move on," Cade said firmly.

She thought that might be a good idea and gingerly stepped over the mess as she followed the tanned Floridian out of the room and into the corridor. They were alone, for now. Each raised their weapons and made their way down the narrow passageway. Halfway along, she heard more shooting and a man screaming. Was that Decker? It sounded like him. Her mind was filled with images of him being hurt, or worse.

"Keep going," Cade said. "It wasn't Mitch. Trust me."

She prayed he was right and kept going. They heard movement behind them and turned to see a man entering the passageway by the same door they had just used. He was crouching down and examining the body of his associate on the floor of the lounge area. He didn't look too happy. He brought his gun up and opened fire on them.

"Cover!" Cade yelled.

Caught in a savage fusillade of automatic gunfire, they each crashed through doors on either side of the corridor and rolled out of the line of fire.

33

Selena hit the carpet face first and skidded to a halt with a painful friction burn on her cheek. Not a good day. Where the hell was she? Looked like one of the yacht's impressive staterooms. Another burst of gunfire and more screaming. She twisted her neck and looked up in time to see Cade Thurman leaping across the corridor and crashing down beside her in a hail of lead.

"Are you insane?" she cried out.

He brushed himself down and smiled at her. "My psychiatrist prefers the term *mildly deranged*."

She laughed. "Yeah, crazy."

They heard the gunman pounding along the corridor and sprinted for cover. Splitting up, Selena ran for a large grand piano and Cade dived behind a sumptuous double bed. The gunman burst into the doorway, gun in his hands, and opened fire again.

The automatic gunfire cut through the air like lightning as he swept the muzzle from side to side and obliterated the hardwood wall above Selena. When he swung the weapon down to where she had landed, she rolled further under the grand piano with only seconds to spare.

The bullets ripped into the Steinway, splintering the hard rock maple into matchwood, striking the music wires, and ricocheting off the Sitka spruce soundboard. A peel of out-of-tune notes rang out in the mayhem.

"Mitch never said you could play the piano, Selena!"

"Such wit," she mumbled under her breath.

From his position behind Danvers's sumptuous double bed, he called out, "Huh?"

"Can we just concentrate on the armed psychopaths and leave the jokes for later when we're in the bar, please Cade?"

He fired on the man, now in the doorway leading out to the foredeck. "*When* we're in the bar? I love an optimist!"

"You sure know how to fill a lady with confidence, Cade Thurman."

The man fired again. Rounds seared through Cade's upper arm. He cried out in pain and dropped his gun.

Selena saw it from under the piano. "Cade!"

*

Decker and Riley ran down to the stern. Entering through a door, they engaged in a short firefight with two armed men in suits. A brief exchange killed one of the men and sent the other retreating into a corridor.

"Go, go, go!" Decker yelled, leading the way with his gun raised into the aim.

He swung into the corridor just in time to see the man dragging Atticus out of one of the cabins. He roughly bundled the old professor in front of him to use as a human shield and fired off another few rounds. Still no sign of Diaz. Decker prayed he was still alive and hit the deck. On his stomach now, arms outstretched before him, he raised his pistol and fired on the man, blowing the top of his skull clean off and spraying the corridor walls with blood and brains.

"Talk about turning someone into pink mist!" Riley yelled. "Good shot, Cap."

As he slumped to the floor, Atticus stepped away and straightened his jacket.

The old bird's as cool as a cucumber, Decker thought, climbing to his knees.

"Ah, Captain Decker!" Atticus said. "How good to see you."

"Are you all right?"

"A little shaken up, but pretty much tip-top as usual."

Decker reloaded. "Then let's get out of here. Hopefully, Lena and the others got the capstone."

Atticus grabbed his elbow and stopped him as he turned to leave. "It's more complicated than that now, Mitch. They have another hostage!"

"We know," Decker said. "A physicist named Salvador Diaz. Why exactly did they want him?"

"They're forcing him to operate the doomsday machine. It's some sort of amplifier. Physics isn't my field at all so it was a bit above my level."

"Mine too, but we can talk about it later," Decker said. "Let's get back to the others."

*

Behind the bed, Cade checked his wound and sighed a breath of relief. Nothing more than a graze, but it had been too close for comfort. Another half-inch and he'd have a lead slug in his arm. "I'm fine," he called back. "Don't worry about it."

"Are you certain?" Selena said.

"Yeah, sure. I love getting shot. I do it all the time."

"With your aim, I can see why…"

"Huh?"

"Nothing… look out!"

The man in the door rushed forward, compact machine pistol held tight to his body as he closed in on Cade behind the bed. At the foot of the bed, he brought his gun up and aimed it at the wounded American. Cade reached out for his dropped gun but he wasn't fast enough. He stared up at the armed man and winced.

The report of the gunshot boomed loudly in the stateroom. He opened his eyes to see the gunman drop to his knees, blood bubbling in spurts from his mouth like a fountain. Then the shot man tipped forward, eyes rolling back in his head, and crashed down into the blood-soaked plush pile.

Selena watched Cade closely as he turned and saw the smoking gun in her hand.

"You're more than welcome, Mr. Thurman."

His heartbeat was like a drum in his chest. "Where the hell did you learn to shoot like that?"

"That's for me to know and you to find out. Right now we have to get out of here! We still haven't found the capstone."

Not exactly sure how he was still alive, Cade snatched up his gun and scrambled out from behind the bed. He trampled over the silk sheets in his filthy, bloody boots and slammed down on the other side, reaching down to help Selena out from behind the trashed piano.

"I'm just going to put myself in serious mode for a second," he said. "Thanks."

She looked down at his blue checked Bermuda shorts and bright sunset-pink Hawaiian shirt.

"You're going to need some new clothes for serious mode, but you're more than welcome."

"Are you and Mitch still an item? Because I sure can see the two of us sharing a sun lounger on Taylor Beach one night."

"I think you'd better keep that thought to yourself, Mr. Thurman. And yes, Mitch and I *are* still an item, as you put it. But I am prepared to do *one* very special thing with you though."

His eyes widened and his heart began to speed up again. "What?"

"Find the frigging capstone!"

"Sure, roger that. But if you ever change your mind..."

"The capstone, Cade! Now!"

With guns held high, they searched the rest of the deck. Quick, quiet, and efficient, they made their way from cabin to cabin. Above their heads, the sound of a desperate gunfight crackled and buzzed. Decker and Riley sounded like they might be in trouble, but she had to put it out of her mind.

"Last cabin on this deck," Selena said. "We're running out of places to search!"

Gun held up into the aim, Cade slowly advanced into the room toward a galvanized steel trunk in the corner. "I think we have it."

"You're counting chickens, Cade."

"Maybe."

Three padlocks secured the trunk. Cade lifted his gun and shot all three locks open in a shower of hot sparks. Then he carefully raised the lid and looked inside.

"Well?" she asked, eyes wide and expectant. "Is it in there?"

"Shoulda waited till the damn chickens hatched, Lena," he said with a sigh. "Sorry."

Selena prayed she was the subject of one of Cade Thurman's notorious gags. When she reached him beside the trunk, she realized that despite the shirt, he was still in serious mode.

"Damn it," she said. "It's not here."

"But it was," he said. "This was definitely the trunk they used to transport the capstone, right?"

She nodded. "I'm sure of it. They obviously got nervous because of our presence on the ship and they've taken it somewhere else."

"And I might know where that is," Atticus said.

Selena turned and saw him standing in the doorway.

Decker and Riley were right behind him.

"Dad!" she cried out and rushed to him. "Are you okay?"

"I'm fine, darling." He wrapped his arms around her and they hugged for a second. "Totally fine. Danvers just wanted me to assist him in his translation of the glyphs on the capstone."

"And the black eye?" she asked.

"I politely declined his offer of employment, at least at first."

She stifled a laugh, but then grew serious. "How could you be so stupid? He might have killed you!"

"He's always stupid!" Decker said.

"Hey! And I thought you were a friend…"

"What's that noise?" Selena asked.

Decker frowned. "What noise?"

"Like an engine," she said.

Riley looked through the porthole and smacked his fist against the bulkhead. "Bugger it! It's the *Holcan's* tender. They're getting away with the capstone!"

34

When they got on deck it was already too late. The ship's powerful tender was racing away from the yacht, complete with the capstone and Professor Diaz.

"To the bridge!" Decker said.

They followed him up to the top deck and quickly reached the yacht's nerve center. Cade fired up the engine and used the wheel to turn the boat's bow away from a mooring pole, rapidly taking the yacht out into the middle of the marina. The Snake King and his men were already nearing the main channel. Now they turned and fired on the *Holcan*.

Bullets ripped into the yacht's fiber-glass hull and punched holes in the windows of the wheelhouse. Cade ducked down behind the wheel and the rest of the Avalon crew dived to the floor and rolled away from the shattered glass spraying all over the bridge. Outside on the jetty, the man they had seen with the marlin turned to flee to the shore but was cut to ribbons by their rounds. He fell dead into the churned-up water.

Cade steered the yacht into a swerving pattern to evade as much of the fire as possible, but the heavy boat was easy to track by the men on the tender.

Decker scrambled to his feet and aimed his gun through the open window. He opened fire on the fleeing tender, aiming at the man at the helm. He missed but hit one of the men firing off the stern. The wounded man crashed into the tender's wake but the Snake King ordered the boat to continue at full speed.

"Don't hit Diaz!" Selena said.

"I can see the damned capstone!" the American yelled.

"So near and yet so far," said Riley, pulling up beside him as he smacked a fresh magazine into the grip of his pistol. "Don't worry, Cap – we'll get it back!"

To their left, Selena was leveling her gun through the open window and taking a few potshots of her own. "Missed."

"You'll get over it," Riley said. "Especially when I teach you how to shoot straight."

"Hey," she shouted. "Anyone ever tell you that you're a very cheeky bastard?"

"I've heard it more than 'good morning', mate. Why?"

Selena laughed. "Maybe take it to heart?"

"And lose the magic that is me? I can't deprive this world of that, mate. Never."

Selena shook her head. "Can any of that magic actually stop Danvers from getting away with my capstone?"

"Our capstone," Riley said.

"Yes, that's what I said."

Cade turned hard to port and the boat tipped. The momentum of the speed and turn made the crew tumble over to the side. Each grabbed something to hang onto. Atticus, from behind them on the soft seats, said, "I think I feel sick…"

"Hey!" Cade yelled. "My driving's not that bad!"

Selena stifled a scream. "And would someone please just take another shot at those guys, they're getting away!"

"It's not that easy," Decker said. "We could hit Diaz!"

"Then aim *carefully*!"

Decker raised his gun and focused. With the tender rapidly tearing away from them in the channel, he raised his gun into the aim and opened fire.

The first shot found its bloody mark. The first struck Diego Novarro in the head, sending him crashing off the side of the speeding tender. The second went off course and punched a neat hole in the gas tank, but failed to ignite the fuel.

"Damn it!" Decker said. "That's what I was talking about. You know how lucky we are that thing didn't explode?"

Gas started spilling out of the hole and running down into the water. How soon the tender ran out of fuel was anyone's guess, but they couldn't count on it. Decker knew firing again could ignite the spilled fuel, and if the boat blew up, not only would Diaz be dead but the heavy metal capstone would be on the seafloor within seconds.

"We're running out of options!" Selena said.

Atticus covered his mouth with his hand. "Is there a sick bag anywhere?"

"We can still catch them in this thing, right?" Decker asked.

Cade nodded. "It's faster than the tender but much less maneuverable. If they continue north into Biscayne Bay they could lose us around some of the artificial islands there."

"That's not going to happen though, right?" Selena asked.

"Not if I can help it."

She raised an eyebrow. "And can you help it?"

"Watch and learn, Professor Moore!"

She smirked at him, but her father turned in his head. "Did someone say my name in vain?"

"I was talking to the other Professor Moore," he said. "Junior."

"I am no one's junior!"

Cade shrugged. "Any way you like it, darlin'."

"And neither am I your...."

Cade spun the wheel and tipped the boat to starboard. Seaspray whipped up in foamy arcs as they plowed over the tender's wake. Selena tipped over and slid down to the floor.

"You did that on purpose!"

"I did not," he said. "They're firing on us! You want us to get shot? I'm taking evasive action."

She got back to her feet and pulled her top straight. "In that case, I forgive you."

Cade shook his head and muttered something under his breath before spinning the wheel back around and teasing the throttles back a little to pull away from the wake.

"They're getting even further away!" Riley shouted.

"Not on my watch," Cade said.

It turned out Cade Thurman's serious mode included the best yacht driving any of the Avalon crew had ever seen. He spun the wheel around and pushed the throttles forward with a cool efficiency before coming around behind the tender. Keeping its wake off to the port side, he powered the massive engines of the Holcan even harder and gave a loud whoop of joy as he punched the air.

"Damn it, I love this thing!"

"We're gaining on them," Atticus said, hanging on to the helm, his face turning green. "This is most exciting. I think I'm starting to love it too, even with the seasickness!"

Cade laughed. "You are gold dust, man. Twenty-four carat."

"Don't speak too soon," Decker said. "Check out the chopper."

Cade and the Avalon crew looked through the yacht's shattered windshield and watched helplessly as a Bell 206 Long Ranger swooped out over the water and hovered above the tender. A rope ladder tumbled out of its side and the Snake King climbed up inside the cabin. Then Tarántula fired on the yacht as the Mercado brothers and

Diablo tied the capstone to a hook-mounted hoist and winched it up inside the aircraft.

"Hurry, Cade!" Selena said. "We can still reach them in time!"

Now, the Mercado brothers forced Diaz up the rope ladder and followed him up. Next was Diablo. Tarántula was last, firing haphazardly on the yacht with one hand as he grabbed hold of the ladder. The chopper rose into the air with him still at the bottom of the ladder, firing on them. Then it swooped down over the causeway and disappeared over Miami's Upper East Side.

Inside the wheelhouse, Decker saw Cade slam his fist down on the helm and curse.

"We lost them!" Selena said.

Cade blew out a breath. "Sorry guys, I screwed up and let them get away."

"No way, mate. A chopper? That's just cheating," Riley said.

Selena watched the Bell recede into the sky over Pelican Island, and with it, her hopes of retrieving the Xunantunich capstone. She wandered outside the bridge and slumped down against the bow rail and felt like crying. "It's over."

"Why is it over?" Atticus said, following her outside.

She turned to her father. "Sorry?"

He gave her a warm smile. "I asked why you said it was over."

"Because Nate Sodding Danvers, the Snake King, just flew away with the capstone in a sodding helicopter and he still has a hostage! That's the end of the chase, Dad! Unless this yacht is so fantastic it has special little wings as well?"

"But we don't need to go after them, my dear!" he said.

All faces, inside and outside the bridge, turned to him, aghast.

"What?" Decker asked through the broken bridge house windshield.

Atticus shuffled his feet, the color gradually returning to his face. "Well..."

Selena's hands were on her hips again. This usually meant trouble. "Dad, why did you just say that?"

He scratched his head and looked sheepish. "Because I know where they're going."

Inside the bridge, Cade kicked the platform of the ship's wheel and cursed. "If you know where they're going, professor, why the hell did we just spend a half hour chasing them up and down Biscayne Bay and getting shot at?"

"I thought maybe it would be a better idea to bring them into custody or something. The sooner or better, as it were. They still have poor Salvador!"

Decker's sigh was covered up by Riley's loud, honest laugh. "Fucking fantastic," the Aussie said. "I love it."

"Into custody?" Cade said. "We're not the coast guard."

"But you were all having so much fun," Atticus said. "I didn't want to spoil it."

"All right," Decker said, unsure exactly what to say. "May I ask where they're taking the capstone?"

"To New York City, of course!" Atticus said. "Danvers is under the impression the only way he can appease Huracan is by destroying the entire city."

"New York," Selena said. "I was afraid of that."

"This is terrible," said Decker. "Nearly twenty million people are living in New York!"

"You have some pretty crazy friends, Professor," Cade said. "Snake kings, Hurricane gods... Jeez. And I thought my friends were nuts because they get smashed and go gator fishing."

"Yes, it appears Danvers is quite out of his mind,"

Atticus said. "Such a shame. He had such a brilliant mind, too."

Decker put his gun in his holster and picked up his hat. Brushing it clean, he put it back on his head and sighed. "He might have had a brilliant mind once, Atticus, but he's well and truly out of it now. We have to stop him before he commits genocide."

"How quickly can the Avalon get us up to New York City, Mitch?" Selena asked.

"Five or six hours."

"Do you know where they're going to set up the capstone in New York?" Riley asked.

"As a matter of fact, I do," Atticus said. "They're planning on using somewhere called the Central Park Tower. Apparently, Danvers bought the penthouse suite there just so he could access the roof without hindrance."

"Then we have a new mission," Decker said. "We fly to New York and get to Central Park Tower as fast as possible."

"But if they're in a private jet they'll be there in under two hours!" Cade said.

"Not exactly," Decker said. "They have to get to an airfield first, then they have to land in an airport in New York. Allow an hour either side of that and we're looking at closer to four hours, plus they have to get across the city to the tower. It's a couple of blocks south of Central Park, meaning the nearest airport is La Guardia. After they land and get out of the airport that's a lot of time burned up in traffic right there."

"But where the hell are *we* going to land?" Cade said.

"We?" said Selena. "That's a trifle presumptuous. Who said you're coming along?"

Cade grinned. "Aw, c'mon! You're not going to make my part in this story end right here, are you?"

She sighed. "Very well, I suppose you have your uses."

"Thanks, man. But what about my question? How the hell are we going to get there first?"

"We might not be able to get there first," Decker said with a grin, "but I sure know a way to cut some corners."

"What does that mean?" Selena asked. "Just what are you planning, Mitch Decker?"

His grin broke into a smile. "I'd tell you, but you'd think I was crazy."

35

New York City

Decker had landed airplanes in a lot of wild places. Rocky Chinese canyons and Indonesian mountain passes. Norwegian fjords and African jungles. Today, he decided to put the Hudson River on his resumé and see how it looked there.

But there were some technical challenges. First, the river was the border between New York and New Jersey and the airspace was busy. Second, to get the best time advantage over the Snake King, he wanted to put her down somewhere in between Union City and Hell's Kitchen. That way they could pull in and moor near the Hudson River Park and go straight down West 57th Street.

And this was a busy stretch of the river. The busy waterway hosted several tour boat companies and private sailing vessels and even some fishing. By this time of day, the river would already be teeming with life and rife with opportunities for disaster. But the good news was, Decker knew seaplanes landed on the Hudson all the time. He dialed into the frequency of the local tower and started talking.

"Tower, this is Albatross niner-seven-four, requesting permission to land on the Hudson."

There was a pause. Static filled the speaker as the controller checked their location on the radar.

"Copy that, turn left heading three-one-zero."

"Three-one-zero."

Decker banked the Avalon gently to the right and watched the nice, fat river line up in front of the aircraft. It was a clear, sunny day and he had been right about the waterborne traffic. Yachts and sailboats were dotted all over the river, bright white dashes on a blue canvas. No problem. Decker had been flying since he was a teenager. After that, he had been trained by and flown for the US Marine Corp. He could land anything anywhere, just so long as the plane was in good working order. He started to relax. No problems here.

A loud explosion rocked the aircraft.

"What the hell was that?" Selena asked.

Decker gave the altimeter a gentle tap and frowned. "Problems. We got problems."

"What sort of problems? Selena asked urgently. "Can they be fixed?"

"Fixed? She has to be finessed. She's a yacht of the air!"

"It's a seaplane, Mitch. It has to be fixed and operated. Fix it and operate it!"

As the aircraft juddered and moaned, Decker huffed out a cynical laugh. "I can see you know *nothing* about old machinery, especially vintage aircraft. The Avalon has more personality than…" he paused to search for a comparison. "Riley here, for example."

"I heard that Cap, and it hurts!" Riley shouted from the main cabin.

Decker pushed on. "You have to treat old machinery with respect, with love. If you do, it will love you right back. Also, technically she's an amphibious flying boat and not a seaplane because she can land on solid ground."

The starboard engine made a deep belching noise and the plane shuddered.

"Damn it," Decker said. "What the hell's the matter with this old pile of…" His voice trailed.

Selena raised an eyebrow. "I'm sorry, what was that last bit, Mitch? I missed it."

"Fine, sometimes she needs a little more TLC than usual. Now is one of those times. I think the repair I made to the shot-up engine back in the jungle might need a little tweaking. That is all."

"A little tweaking? Are we safe or not?"

"More or less."

"More or less!"

"Just take it easy. I'm going to bring her in and land on the river just like we planned. Everything is going to be just fine. You can thank me later."

Selena looked outside as New Jersey rushed past the portside window. "Thank God."

"Yeah, just fine," Decker muttered. "Probably."

*

The Snake King watched Tarántula and his men fuss around the capstone as they worked to lift the strange, heavy metal pyramid into position high on top of Central Park Tower. Years of patient planning were slowly coming together right before his very own eyes. It was almost impossible to contain his excitement, but he hadn't reached his full destiny.

Much was left to do, including deleting most of New York City from the map. Only an attack of this magnitude would demonstrate to the American authorities that he had the power to destroy any part of their empire at a whim. After that came the blackmail and then the biggest payoff in history.

"Is it ready, Diaz?" he snapped.

The old Cuban professor fussed around inside the capstone. "Almost."

"Good. I am impatient to show my devotion to the

mighty Huracan."

He closed his eyes and heard the voices of the ancient past. Maya priests summoning gods, the sound of the frenzied worshippers, and then the roar of the gods themselves. Only the reincarnated souls of the ancient priests could possibly experience such vivid memories. He knew he was such a man, deep in his heart. The colors and the sounds swirled in his mind. He felt the mighty power of a host of unknown gods shake the very ground he was standing on.

"Professor Diaz," he said, opening his eyes. "Is it ready yet? I am running out of patience."

"Yes," he said. "It is ready, and may God forgive me for the part I have played in this disgrace."

The Snake King laughed loudly. "Your weak and pathetic God may forgive, but mine will not. All praise the mighty Huracan!"

He stepped forward, removed the Huracan idol, and activated the device. Instantly, they felt it drawing electromagnetic waves up through the skyscraper and gathering power. The building began to rumble and clouds started to swirl above their heads.

"Start the chopper, Tarántula!"

"Boss."

"When this gets up to full power, we don't want to be anywhere near this city."

"I'm on my way."

"You're insane!" Diaz yelled, his hair whipping across his face in the gathering storm. "Crazy!"

The Snake King calmly fitted his jade mask and laughed loudly. "Huracan!" he screamed into the sky. "Huracan! Destroy this corrupt and wicked city!"

*

Smoke poured from the starboard engine as Decker brought the slab-sided seaplane around and finished the turn. Then, he reduced power to the mighty Wright R-1820 Cyclone radial engines. He was judging their power by the hum but he checked it by reading the instrument panel. Extended flaps. The airplane descended like a feather, then some turbulence buffeted them up and down for a moment.

"One hundred above."

Less power, engines down almost to idle.

Fifty, forty, thirty...

With a sailing boat on the port side and a tour boat on their starboard, he touched down on the surface. The deep-V hull sliced into the water like a hot knife through butter. Great arcs of water sprayed either side of the plane and into the air in frothy white jets. The aircraft juddered and rattled as the friction of the water against the hull slowly dragged them down to a crawl.

"Tower, be advised we're down on the water."

The controller directed him to moor the Avalon on the east bank. He had landed on the Jersey side of the river and gently steered the old bird to the east. The famous Manhattan skyline slowly turned into view as he slowed the revs further and then killed the engines.

Riley had already popped up in the forward hatch just in front of the cockpit. He was holding the plane's boat hook, which he now pushed out into the water. Hooking the end around a mooring buoy, he pulled it back in. Then he grabbed the loop at the end of the heavy rope and lashed it to the mooring hook on the aircraft's nose. As the plane drifted in closer to the shore, Charlie hopped out and ran along the jetty, further securing the plane to a mooring pole.

They were officially in New York City.

Out of the plane and over Twelfth Avenue. Traffic was

busy and they weaved in and out of the cars and trucks on foot but with weapons concealed. Horns blew, drivers shouted, and waved fists. Diana apologized with a wave. Charlie tried to explain. Riley laughed. Then they were on 57th Avenue. From the far western end of the avenue, they could already see the colossal sight of Central Park Tower. The giant glass and steel structure rose up from the busy and expensive block in between Seventh and Eighth Avenues.

They were already crossing Eleventh Avenue. "Just another three blocks to go!" Decker said.

"And then about another block vertically, by the look of that tower!" said Diana.

Riley laughed. "I think it's probably got elevators."

"It's got elevators," Decker said.

They ran on, dodging pedestrians ambling along the sidewalks. Another busy day in Midtown Manhattan, Decker thought. He hated this place. He was a country boy, from Monroe County upstate New York. That was where he learned to fly, in a reconditioned Tiger Moth. If he wanted nightlife, the busy streets of Rochester were enough for him. This place was just *crazy*.

"Nearly there!"

Selena's voice. He turned and watched her run beside him. Yeah, he was good at landing things, but how a guy like him had landed a woman like her was something he would never understand.

"And we're here, folks!" Riley yelled. "Buckle up for big laughs."

They looked up the front façade of the enormous skyscraper and saw angry, dark black clouds gathering just above the large steel spire. They began to form into a ring, and then another and another until several concentric circles of the clouds expanded above the building.

Acosta simply stared and whistled. "Are we too late?"

"It's like what we saw back in Miami!" Diana said.

Decker looked at the clouds and frowned. "Only this time the clouds are about ten times bigger. This is going to be bad."

"We have to get up there in a hurry, mate!" Riley said, staring up at the gathering electrical storm. But when he turned back to the American, he had already left his side and was running toward the building's main entrance.

36

Decker burst into the lobby. "Get to a shelter! Everyone get to safety, now!"

Dozens of people stopped what they were doing and turned to look at him, a mixture of confusion, fear, and ridicule on their faces. A large man in a security guard uniform strolled over slowly and raised his palms to calm them.

"What the hell is going on here, buddy?"

Selena was now alongside Decker. "We have to get everyone out of this building! They need to get to a shelter."

"Who are you people?"

"I'm Professor Selena Moore."

"Means jack to me, lady."

"I'll have you know good sir that I am a very respected archaeologist!"

He shrugged.

"Listen, there are some men on the roof," Decker said. "They have some sort of device."

The guard's eyes widened. "Are you reporting a bomb?"

"Well..."

The guard was already thumbing the push-to-talk button on the two-way radio fixed to his shoulder.

Decker said, "Not a bomb, exactly, but something much more dangerous."

The guard was listening to him and simultaneously speaking into the radio. "This is Charlie Echo Five calling from the lobby."

"Go ahead, Frank," said a bored voice through the static.

"We have a possible situation here. Some people have entered the lobby in a big hurry claiming there are terrorists on the roof with some sort of bomb."

"What the hell?"

"That's what they say."

"And who the hell are these people?"

"One of them says she's an astrologer."

"An astrologer?" said the voice.

Selena put her hands on her hips. "An archaeologist!"

"Whatever the hell you are, you're not going anywhere until the police arrive."

"What about the men on the roof?"

"You want me to go up to the roof, boss?"

"No. You stay in the lobby. I'll send a team up to check it out," the voice said.

"Copy that."

"They're dangerous," Charlie said. "Your men are going to get killed."

"And we need to get the people out of this lobby!" Selena said. "The entire city needs to be evacuated."

"Evacuate New York City?" the guard started laughing. "Now I *know* you're not being serious."

"I am being serious! At the very least the city needs to be warned there is a very powerful hurricane on the way."

"A hurricane?"

"That's what is on the roof," Acosta said. "A device which creates hurricanes."

"True story, old chap," Atticus said. "Seen it with me very own peepers."

"Damn straight," said Cade with a wide grin.

"Okay, sure there is," the guard said in reassuring tones. "Why don't you sit down over there and one of your friends can get you a cup of coffee, or perhaps even a straight-jacket?"

Selena felt the frustration rising inside her, then Riley tapped him on the shoulder.

Before he had twisted his head around fully, the young Australian delivered an eye-watering headbutt into his face and knocked him out cold.

"Damn!" said Cade. "That's gonna leave a mark."

"Sorry," Riley shrugged. "But that convo was sort of getting a bit circular."

Decker and Charlie were already behind the guard, catching him before he collapsed to the floor and then pulling him over to a couch where they took off his cap and laid it over his face. Diana finished the scene by sliding a large, potted yucca plant around in front of him and blocking him from view.

"What now?" the Portuguese woman said.

"Now, we go to the roof," said Decker.

They sprinted over to the front desk and Charlie drew his gun. Pointing it at a young woman, he smiled. "Terribly sorry about this, but you need to sound whatever alarm system you have in this building."

She stared at the gun, terrified.

Charlie smiled again. "Don't worry about the gun, it's really just for effect. But activate the alarm system. Now. Get people away from windows and any outside areas and into the interior staircases and any storm shelters you might have."

"Er…"

"Now, please."

"But my boss…"

"I don't like to be crass," he said, looking at the gun, "but right now you should think of me as your boss."

She tapped something on her keyboard and an alarm started to sound in the lobby.

"Done."

"Is this sounding through the entire building?"

"Sure. You're not going to shoot me, are you?"

"No, but I might ask you out on a date. See, my name's Charlie Valentine and I work in a team of treasure hunters. I'm sort of their fixer. Indispensable, really. I'm here to stop an insane maniac who thinks he's a Maya snake king destined to summon Huracan into the modern world and destroy civilization. Now, about that date, if you're free..."

She looked confused. "Er...I'm kind of seeing someone."

"Oh, what a pity. We could still do dinner one night, if you're free, then..."

"Charlie!" It was Selena. "Here, now!"

"Sorry, that's the boss. Gotta run. Shame about the dinner. Oh, and keep the elevators running! We have to get to the penthouse."

"Er... sure, I think?"

"Good stuff!"

He joined Selena and the others as they piled into an elevator and hit the penthouse button.

"Very smooth, Charles," Selena said. "Hitting on someone in the middle of a terror attack."

The elevator came to a sudden, unexpected stop.

"Why are we stopping?" Diana asked.

The doors slid open to reveal a wholesome family standing in front of them. Selena saw the look on their faces as they registered the big, ugly gun in her hand. She pushed the gun into her jacket pocket and gave them her best disarming smile. Being in a confined space with your three young kids when a bunch of heavily armed strangers suddenly appeared in view was not ideal, she knew.

"Going up?" Riley asked with a smile.

"I think we'll wait..."

"Get into an interior stairwell as fast as you can,"

Decker said. "And as low as you can in the building. There's a major hurricane about to hit."

The woman looked confused. "A hurricane? At this time of year?"

The former marine leaned forward and pushed the button to close the doors. As they slid to a close, he looked her in the eye. "Just do it, now."

Their next stop was the penthouse. When the doors opened, it didn't take long for their welcoming committee to open fire on them. On the carpet in front of the elevator, they saw Frank's security detail, filled with bullet holes.

"Get down!" Decker yelled.

Riley was ready, tucking himself behind the cabin operating panel and opening fire. A long, sustained burst of accurate fire took out the two men fighting alongside Diablo and drove him back along the corridor.

"He's mine!" Decker yelled.

"Typical Mitch," mumbled Cade. "Glory hog."

Selena watched Decker sprint up the corridor in pursuit of Diablo and darted out after him. The Mexican gangster was already at the far end, grabbing at a door handle. She pushed her legs faster to catch up with the former US marine pilot just as he reached Diablo. The gangster wrenched open the door and jumped into an adjoining room, twisting his upper body around as he ran and lifting his gun into the aim.

"Down!" Decker yelled.

Selena couldn't see past Decker to see for herself why he had told her to get down, but there was no need. After so many adventures and close-calls together, she knew she could trust him in an emergency situation. She dived down, hitting the corridor's carpeted floor at the same time as Decker just as Diablo's gun exploded and sent a bullet tracing inches over her head.

The round punched a hole in the safety glass of a door

at the other end of the corridor. She screamed and covered her head, peering through a gap in her arms just in time to see the Mexican running to the next door. He laughed and raised his gun a second time.

"Cover!" Decker called out and rolled behind an antique chest covered in old books.

Selena copied what he did and found herself behind a heavy wooden bookshelf.

"Are you okay?" Decker called out.

"Yes... at least I think so! That one nearly hit me. Where is he now? Can you see?"

"Yeah, I can see under the chest. He just left the corridor and went into another room. He has nowhere else to run."

"That makes him even more dangerous, Mitch!"

Decker peered over the chest. "I see him!"

He fired and hit Diablo in the back three times. The bullets buried themselves between his shoulder blades, shattering the bone and digging deep inside his lungs. The Mexican gangster went down hard, not even having time to reach out with his hands to soften his fall. His face plowed into the plush pile, and the rest of him came crashing down a second later, dead on touchdown.

"That's another one down," Charlie said. "Now for the others."

37

Decker had paused on the landing not far from Diablo's cooling corpse. A narrow window threw some dull light on the carpet. He walked over to it and saw they were now on the north side, overlooking Central Park. The endless citizens of Midtown Manhattan were innocently going about their business, spending their days without a care in the world. And not a hint of the horrors the Snake King had in store for them.

A deep, violent roar shook the building.

"What the hell was that?" said Diana.

"Looks like Danvers is powering up the Stormbringer," Decker said.

Selena ran to his side and peered over the window ledge. For now, they both saw only order and peace, but they each knew how quickly this would fall apart if they failed to stop the Snake King and his men. If they had learned one thing since their hunt for Shambhala, it was how thin the fabric of polite society was, and how easily it could be torn apart by a man like Nathaniel Danvers.

Far below, a couple of cop cars cruised past, no lights, no sirens. Just driving around waiting for the next dispatcher to call them to a job. A fire truck trundled north on Seventh Avenue, again no hurry at all. Maybe they were going back to their station after a job somewhere south. Pedestrians were slowly starting to notice the clouds. Some pointed and stared but most were still unaware. For now. Decker tried to imagine what a hurricane several magnitudes stronger than the wildest Category Five storms, would be like. He saw it ripping through the city and shredding all of this civilization to pieces before spitting out into the Upper Bay.

"C'mon, let's get on with it," he said. "It's up to us now."

"Next time we do this, someone please talk me out of it!" Charlie said.

"There's not going to be a next time," Selena said.

Decker was already three steps up the next staircase. Now he stopped and looked at her. "What does that mean? You're throwing him off the team?"

"Not exactly."

"Then what?"

"We'll talk about it later, Mitch! We have to stop Danvers!"

He was already running back up the steps to the penthouse's top floor. "You think I don't know that? You think I'm some kind of idiot? We're running up the stairs to get a man who calls himself the Snake King and then you go and drop another cryptic hint about the Avalon team not having a 'next time'!"

"Hey," Charlie said, pounding up the stairs with a gun in his hand. "We're just talking about a short break, right?"

"I'm not talking about it *at all!*" Selena said, struggling not to lose her breath. "I'm focussing on stopping a barking mad apeshit wackadoodle who thinks he's descended from the lizard kings from wiping out twenty million people!"

"Hey, haven't I heard that somewhere before?" Riley asked.

"Keep running, Carr!" Selena said, rapidly running out of breath. "If I don't make it, this could all be down to you."

"Heaven help us," Decker said. "Imagine the fates of twenty million innocent people resting in the hands of a man whose claim to fame is farting the Australian national anthem."

"Don't knock it till you've tried it, Mitch," Riley said. "It raises a real good laugh with the boys from the regiment, every single time."

"Look out!" Diana yelled, pointing ahead.

They had turned into the main room of the penthouse, and now Miguel Mercado was standing on the mezzanine with a submachine gun in each hand. He screamed in Spanish until he was hoarse and opened fire, sweeping the two muzzles in opposite directions and spraying the entire room with hot lead. The mezzanine's smoked glass panels blew into thousands of pieces and rained down over the floorboards below, sending the crew scuttling for cover wherever they could find it.

Selena crashed down behind a long cream couch positioned just in front of the long window wall and cradled her head in her arms. Outside, she saw the storm ripping across the city. It had gained in strength by several magnitudes since they had entered the building and was ferociously beating on the glass and howling like a demon.

"We haven't got much longer!" she cried out. "It's gaining power!"

"I can see that!" Decker called back from behind another chair.

Riley and Charlie were behind them both, having taken up a defensive position behind an enormous central fireplace. Both men now leaned out either side of the chunky steel and brick structure and returned fire, tearing Miguel Mercado to pieces as he screamed and ranted on the mezzanine. His bullet-riddled body tumbled over the steel rail and crashed down on top of a grand piano, snapping the lid prop like a matchstick and smashing the lid and music rack down with a crash.

"Three down," Riley said, sharing a high five with Charlie.

More shots. They jumped and spun around, raising guns into the aim. Charging out of a large bar area, an enraged Carlos Mercado had seen his brother's violent death and was hunting for revenge. He was screaming like a madman and gripping an MP5, firing long bursts and sweeping the weapon from side to side as he covered the penthouse in lead.

Riley had taken a defensive position behind a long leather couch. He moved like lightning, raising his pistol and planting a round in the center of Carlos's face. He followed the attack up with two rounds to his chest and sent him crashing back into a rack of glasses and vodka bottles behind him. Dead before he hit the floor, the big man from Mexico City crashed down like a felled tree, crunching to a stop in a carpet of shattered glass and spilled spirits, the silent MP5 still gripped in his hand.

"Four down," said the Australian.

"Last stop is the roof," Decker said. "Those suffering from vertigo need not apply."

38

Exhausted, cut, bruised, and weary, they accessed a utility corridor via a fire door on the apartment's top floor. Following a bare concrete passageway for a few seconds, they soon reached another door fitted with a chunky steel panic bar. Booting it open with one kick, Riley was through in a flash, gun raised and ready to kill.

But his gun remained cool. "All clear," he said, raising his voice to be heard over the howling gale raging outside. "It's some sort of bulkhead. The roof must be accessed by that other door over there."

"Then let's get on it!" Decker kicked open the panic bar on the other door and they were on the roof. "There!" he yelled. The wind whipped his hat off and blew it clear off the skyscraper. "I see them over there!"

He pointed to the far side of the roof where the Snake King, Tarántula, and Professor Salvador Diaz were standing around the device. The wind was tearing and tugging at them, but seemed less violent near the capstone.

Diaz saw them and made a break for it. The Snake King ordered Tarántula to fire on him and bring him down. Tarántula obeyed, leveling his gun and aiming it squarely at the back of the physicist as he sprinted toward Decker and Selena.

"Mitch!" Selena cried out. "They're going to kill him!"

The wind whipped and tugged at Decker as he aimed his gun at Tarántula and fired. The shot hit him in the upper arm and dropped him to the floor, but he was still in action. He crawled away behind an air-conditioning unit and took cover. Behind him, the Snake King saw what was unfolding and dived behind the capstone. Drawing his weapon, both he and Tarántula returned fire on the Avalon crew.

Bullets crisscrossed through the air and shattered a row of windows in the side of one of the bulkheads in the center of the roof. Decker covered his face to shield it from the flying shards of glass. Selena threw herself to the ground and rolled behind one of the air-conditioning units. Up ahead of them, Riley, Charlie, and Cade were splitting up and trying to attack the Snake King on three fronts. Diana, Atticus, and Acosta were still inside the bulkhead, their heads tucked down into their bodies to avoid the flying glass.

"Go, Charlie!" Riley called out. "Go, go, go!"

The former military cop charged toward the Snake King's position, using the chopper for cover before sliding to a stop just under its tail boom. Riley had taken up an offensive position on the other side of the roof not far from Cade. They were using large electrical access boxes for cover. Decker had to move forward from another direction and put more pressure on Danvers. Spying a large water tank on the building's south side, he leaned over to Selena.

"You think you can get to that tank?"

"Anything you can do, Mitch..."

He grinned. "I know, I know... you can do better."

"You got it."

He turned to Diana, Atticus, and Acosta. "What about you?"

They shook their heads. "I don't think so, Mitch," Atticus said. "I think this is all a bit out of our league."

Decker understood. "Then stay here, and when we go, lock the bulkhead door behind us and make sure the panic bar is firmly back in position. We don't know how this is going to pan out, but if it ends up with us taking out their chopper and them trying to make a break for it down these stairs, I don't want you in a vulnerable position."

"But how will you get back in?" Diana asked. "How will we know it's you?"

"You'll know," he said with a smile. "Ready, Lena?"

"I've been ready since you told me about the water tank."

"Then let's go!"

By the time they reached the tank, the Snake King had got into the chopper and was powering up the engine. He lifted the aircraft off the roof and rotated it in the air. Decker watched the wind throwing it around and guessed old Danvers had planned to be far away by the time the winds had reached this velocity.

Tarántula called out to him but he turned away and flew in the opposite direction. The wounded Mexican gangster broke cover and ran after him, reaching out with his bloody arms as he desperately tried to grab hold of one of the skids.

"He's crazy!" Riley yelled.

Charlie and Cade fired on the chopper, missing by inches. "They're both crazy!"

Tarántula grabbed the skid just as the chopper flew over the edge of the skyscraper. Riley fired and hit him in the back, forcing him to release his grip on the skid and fall screaming from the chopper. A few meters beneath the aircraft the wind caught hold of him and clawed him away at high speed. Decker watched in horror as the wind tipped the chopper on its side and sliced Tarántula in two with its rotors. Both halves of the gangster tumbled away in the swirling maelstrom as the Snake King struggled to right the chopper.

It was no good. The power of the wind was too much

for the aircraft. It lost all stability and turned upside down before losing lift and tumbling down the side of the skyscraper. Decker and the others ran to the rail and leaned over the edge just in time to see the storm catch hold of the chopper one more time and throw it into the skyscraper on the other side of the street. It exploded in a ball of fire and dropped like a stone to the street below, streaking a long line of burning oil and flames and smoke in its wake.

"My God!" Diana said a prayer in whispered Portuguese.

Charlie and Cade shared a high five while Riley released his empty mag and replaced it with a new one, holstering the weapon. Selena turned away from the burning wreckage plummeting through the stormy air and shook her head.

Decker holstered his gun and turned to the Cuban professor. "Get that damned thing turned off, Diaz!"

"On my way!"

Decker was searching the roof for something. "And where the hell is my hat?"

EPILOGUE

The following day's dawn broke hot and humid. A thunderstorm was gathering power just off to the west and by the time the crew met for breakfast, all dressed in shorts and t-shirts, it had already started to rain over the city. Their hotel's breakfast room was situated on the east side of the building with an impressive, panoramic view of Midtown Manhattan and despite the bad weather, people were still walking along the street, shopping, working, some even jogging.

No one in the Avalon crew had the energy for any of that today. Not even Riley. Instead, they shuffled around the self-service buffet tables and piled their plates full of food. Atticus and Charlie and Cade stuck with plain, black coffee and toast with grape jelly. Diana, Acosta, and Diaz chose mostly fruit and some healthy cereal with skim milk. Selena was happy with a single cup of tea with a dash of milk and some brioche with Chantilly cream. Riley and Decker had opted for a chunky omelet with green onions and Swiss cheese, washed down with hot black coffee.

As they shuffled back over to their table by the window and took their seats, Atticus was the first to speak.

"Bloody good breakfast, here. I do like this purple jam."

Cade laughed. "We call it grape jelly. Purple jam. Pure gold dust, man."

Selena rolled her eyes.

"What?" Atticus asked his daughter.

"All you ever think about is your stomach, Dad."

"And what else is there to think about?"

"That we almost died yesterday!"

"*Almost*, Lena," he said cheerily. "That is the operative word. Almost. Ooh, real butter!"

She looked to Decker for sympathy and maybe found a little lurking at the back of his eyes.

"Atticus is right," Decker said. "We might have *almost* died, but we didn't. We survived and Nathaniel Danvers and his gang are all dead, including the men holding Cristina Diaz down in Havana."

"And thank you all for that," Diaz said. "You saved my family from endless suffering and pain."

"It's over now," Selena said. "As Mitch says, Danvers is gone."

"And Danvers was quite insane," Salvador Diaz said. "Not only did he think he was doing Huracan's bidding, but he also believed he was seeing the future when he looked into the capstone."

"Wasn't he?" Selena asked.

Diaz laughed. "Not at all. The capstone is made from a very mysterious metal I have never encountered before. Danvers told me he called it *divinium*, mostly because of his insane god complex, I should think."

A gentle laugh rippled around the breakfast table.

Diaz continued. "I had plenty of chance to study this new metal when he was forcing me to operate the device, and what I found was intriguing. As is now obvious, the metal was an unimaginably powerful conductor, unlike any other, I have studied. More than that, it grew intensely hot when in use and gave off fumes. This is a well-known phenomenon we've known about for a long time, and it induces in anyone too close to it something called metal fume fever. I recognized it at once so I kept my distance, but Danvers had no idea what was really happening. This caused him to have vivid hallucinations based on his innermost fears."

"So he wasn't seeing the future at all?" Diana asked.

"I really don't think so," he said with an intriguing smirk. "Why, do you?"

A tense silence was followed by relieved laughter, then Decker said, "So, Lena... Earlier in the mission, you told everyone you had something important to tell us about the future of the Avalon crew. Later, when we were in Central Park Tower, you said there wasn't going to be a next time for the Avalon crew. I think I speak for everyone when I say, we're all ears."

"Fine," she said in clipped tones. She dabbed at the corners of her mouth with a linen napkin and dropped it on the table, lifting her chin proudly like a medieval princess. "I think it's time we disbanded for a while."

Everyone stopped what they were doing and stared at her.

"Whoa, mic drop!" Cade said.

"Huh?" Riley said. "What do you mean?"

"I mean, I think we should go on a break," she continued.

Decker gently set down his fork with some untouched omelet on it and looked at her earnestly. "You're serious?"

"I am."

"But why?" Charlie asked.

"We're not professional treasure hunters, Charlie, that's why. You nearly went into a coma in Cuba. We all nearly died here in New York and the only reason we didn't was pure luck."

"I'm former SAS!" Riley said. "We make our own luck!"

"And I'm an ex-US Marine," Decker put in. "It wasn't luck that saved us."

"But I'm a museum curator," she said. "And my father

is just an archaeologist too, and getting on in years."

"I say, steady on Lena!" Atticus said. "I'm not ready for the knacker's yard just yet."

"And you'll get there sooner than you think if we carry on like this!" she snapped. "And think about Diana! She's a linguist, for heaven's sake. What we're doing is just crazy. Sooner or later, one of us *will* get killed doing this and I don't want that on my conscience. This is why I feel we should take a bit of time out to reconsider what the Avalon crew is really all about."

"She has a point," Diana said. "Since I joined the crew, my career has taken a real hit."

"But you get paid for working with us," Riley said. "We all do. To the victor go the spoils, and we divide them fairly among us."

"It's not just that, Riley," she said. "As a linguist, I have a reputation within the academic community. Flying around the world is fun, but scary and I am not a very brave person. I agree with Lena. I think we should go back to our lives for a little while and take stock."

Riley scratched his head and stuffed a chunk of the omelet in his mouth. He shrugged and mumbled something through the mouthful of egg.

"Charlie?" Selena asked. "What do you think?"

He also shrugged. "I think it was a great ride but if this is what you want then that's just fine with me. There's always work for me over in Thailand. Call me when you need me."

She looked at Decker. "What about you, Mitch?"

"What about me?"

"Do you agree a break might be good for us?"

"Do you mean a break from what we do in the Avalon crew, or do you mean a break from the two of us?"

She rolled her eyes. "Let's not be melodramatic, darling. I meant the team."

He paused. "In that case, come with me."

Everyone stopped eating and watched Decker take Selena's hand as he walked her away from the table.

*

It didn't take long for the elevator to reach the top of the Empire State Building. Stepping out onto the 102nd floor's brand new observatory, Decker walked to the enormous window and gazed over Manhattan. It was a breathtaking view. The sun broke through a hole in the clouds and reflected off the East River. Behind them, some tourists snapped photos through the polished glass.

Selena sighed happily. "An impressive city."

"I agree," Decker said. "And I say that as a proud New Yorker."

"Wait a minute. You said you were an Upstater and that you hated the city."

"Sure, but I'm still a New Yorker. Besides, one of my grandmothers was born on the Upper West Side. It counts."

She grinned and gave him a sideways glance. "All right, I'll let you off *this* time."

"Good, because I wanted to ask you a question."

"Oh yeah? What sort of question?"

Looking out over the Manhattan morning, Decker turned the little box over in his pocket. With Selena and him it had not exactly been love at first sight, but now he couldn't imagine being without her. He had made up his mind. He pulled the box out of his pocket and held it up between them. Opening it, he saw her eyes widen and her mouth fell open a little.

She brought her hands up to her mouth and widened her eyes in shock. "Oh my God!"

Decker shuffled around, blocking the view of the

moment from a handful of tourists behind them. "Professor Moore, will you marry me?"

She looked into his eyes and stood on her tiptoes to kiss him on the mouth.

"I think we both know the answer to that, Captain Decker."

THE END

AUTHOR'S NOTE

So comes an end to another successful mission for the intrepid crew of the Avalon. I hope you enjoyed reading it as much as I always enjoy researching and writing about these exotic locales, not to mention the wonderful old treasures and legends. I tried to make this a leaner, faster adventure for the crew, and I hope you think I made that work.

A fourth adventure for the crew may be on the cards for 2021 but the next release will be the big one – *Shadow of the Apocalypse* (Joe Hawke 15). In this latest outing, Hawke and the rest of our beleaguered heroes end the nightmare they have been plunged into and prepare for a brand new life – and some very different adventures. I'm aiming for an autumn 2020 release on this one. Following this will be *The Titanic Mystery* (Hunter Files 3), slated for November/December 2020.

Until next time Dear Mystery Reader,

Rob

ABOUT THE AUTHOR

Rob Jones has published 25 international Kindle bestsellers, including the Joe Hawke series, the Hunter Files, the Avalon Adventures, the Cairo Sloane series, the Raiders series, the Harry Bane Thriller series, the DCI Jacob mysteries and his brand new action thriller *The Operator*. Originally from the United Kingdom, today he lives in Australia with his wife and children.

Printed in Great Britain
by Amazon

61937537R00139